The New
BLACK
MASK
QUARTERLY

The New BLACK MASK QUARTERLY

Number 1

EDITED BY

MATTHEW J. BRUCCOLI & RICHARD LAYMAN

A HARVEST/HBJ BOOK

HARCOURT BRACE JOVANOVICH, PUBLISHERS

SAN DIEGO   NEW YORK   LONDON

Editorial correspondence should be directed to the editors at: Bruccoli Clark Publishers, Inc., 2006 Sumter Street, Columbia, SC 29201.

Designed by G. B. D. Smith

Printed in the United States of America

ISBN 0-15-665479-2

First Harvest/HBJ edition 1985

A B C D E F G H I J

HBJ

Contents

Introduction

The New Black Mask Quarterly is an expression of homage to the original *Black Mask* pulp magazine which flourished in the twenties and thirties and provided an incubator for the hard-boiled school of writing. Whether—as literary historians have claimed—those writers really established the authentic voice of American prose, it is indisputable that American fiction would be very different without the progeny of Dashiell Hammett and Raymond Chandler. This extended family includes Ross Macdonald, John D. MacDonald, Mickey Spillane, Horace McCoy, James M. Cain, Robert B. Parker, and Elmore Leonard.

Black Mask died a lingering death in 1951. The crumbling copies are now collector's items and have the look of literary artifacts. Yet the tradition remains vital. Under its most influential editor, Joseph T. Shaw (1926-1936), *Black Mask* achieved a wide reputation for strong fiction; in that respect we will endeavor to emulate our namesake. But *The New Black Mask Quarterly* will not be restricted to hard-boiled detective stories. Classifiers enjoy differentiating among the detective story, the mystery story, the crime story, the suspense story, and what the British designate the "thriller." Our pages will be open to all of these categories, as well as spy fiction. Since British writers have always been masters of the mystery, their work will be sought—with the exception of what has been called the "murder-in-ye-olde-quaint-cottage-story," against which the original *Black Mask* boys reacted.

We dispute authorities such as W. H. Auden, who have insisted that mystery and suspense stories are meant to be purely escapist. This generalization obtains if it is restricted to plot. We believe that good ficition is remembered for its characters. The "whodunit" label is respectable when the first syllable is accented.

We undertook this series at the invitation of William Jovanovich, who provided the editorial rationale. Although *The New Black Mask Quarterly* will reprint buried stories that extend the tradition of the hard-boiled movement, our brief is not to resurrect the founding fathers, but to publish the best fiction we can obtain from the present generation of mystery and thriller writers.

—The Editors

The New

BLACK MASK

QUARTERLY

Robert B. Parker:
An Interview

This is the first of a series of features to be presented in NBMQ on contemporary masters of mystery and suspense fiction. Robert B. Parker has been chosen as our first subject because he is the preeminent hard-boiled detective writer to emerge since the 1970s.

Parker has overcome the limitations of genre fiction. He has achieved recognition among book reviewers and literary critics as a significant voice in American fiction whose characters deal sensitively and realistically with complex moral issues. After earning a Ph.D. in literature Robert Parker worked as a university professor for fifteen years, writing in his spare time. The Godwolf Manuscript, the first novel featuring his series detective, Spenser, was published in 1973; six years and six novels later, Parker gave up teaching to write full time. The publication in 1985 of The Catskill Eagle will be Parker's twelfth Spenser novel.

The following interview was conducted by phone on January 7, 1985. Parker was preparing for a reception held that evening by the Governor of Massachusetts to welcome the television crew who will be shooting a made-for-TV movie adapted from Promised Land.

NBMQ: You have been called the modern voice of the hard-boiled detective novel. Do you resent, as Hammett and Chandler did, being classified that way?

Parker: No. To say no is a little misleading. I don't

pay much attention to categories, one way or another. I think they are useful—and I mean this in no pejorative way—for everybody but writers. They are useful for critics, librarians, booksellers, and people who have to file and catalogue and organize. When I go to a bookstore to look for a novel by Stephen King, I want to look under fantasy or science fiction or whatever rather than have to go through the whole bookstore alphabetically. But when I write, I'm doing the same process that, say, William Faulkner did. The difference between us is not that I'm writing a hard-boiled novel; the difference is that Faulkner wrote better than I do, and wrote better than I ever will, probably. Because categories are of no real consequence to me, I don't think in those terms. I neither resent nor not resent them.

NBMQ: One critic has suggested that you are better able to handle serious themes by incorporating them into a mystery novel.

Parker: I think he's probably right. Whether that would be true of other writers I don't know, but in my case the mystery form gives me the kind of structure in which I work. I would not be able to explain why that is so exactly, if I were pressed. But I have a sense that it probably is so. Rather than constricting me, the form allows me a kind of freedom. Was it Ross Macdonald who compared the novel to a sonnet in its structure? I don't have a sense as I write a novel that I am required to do anything because I am writing hard-boiled detective fiction. I suppose that certain common sense decisions have been made—like not to kill Spenser in the middle of the second novel. But those are not artistic; those are common sense decisions.

NBMQ: Ross Macdonald has said the detective story is like a welder's mask in that it enables the writer to deal with material that is too hot for other contexts.

Parker: I don't think so, but it may be. He spoke very beautifully about detective fiction. But I've always found it a little hard to figure out what he meant by what he said. It's one of those nice quotes that sounds good. He also said the detective was so thin that you could barely see him; that he was interested in other people. When I read Macdonald I am interested in Archer much more than the other characters. It always seemed to me that the novels were about him.

NBMQ: The term "hard-boiled" is abused so much today that it has almost lost its meaning. And yet, certainly there is a hard-boiled tradition at work. The influence of Hammett and Chandler is obvious.

Parker: Oh, hell. Hemingway was of the hard-boiled tradition. It doesn't have to be about a detective to be hard-boiled. It's in many ways the post-World War I tradition of American fiction. There is a kind of hard-boiledness to *The Great Gatsby*.

NBMQ: What have you brought to this tradition to make it different from the way it was when Hemingway and Chandler and Hammett wrote?

Parker: Love. I write about love, and I don't think any of them did. Much of what I write about is about love. The relationship between Spenser and Susan, the relationship between parents and children, the

3

relationship between husbands and wives. I would guess that the good news is that not many people have been doing that. One estimable person said I do it better than anyone now writing. Another estimable person said that the plots between Susan and Spenser should be sub-plots, but they become major plots and that damages my work. So you can take either one you want. If I have changed the form, whatever that form quite is, I think it's because of the degree to which I use it as a vehicle to write about love, which certainly not many hard-boiled private detective writers do. There's not much American fiction about love.

NBMQ: As a trained literary historian, if not literary critic, what do you think of the way the literary critics and reviewers have served you? Have they been perceptive?

Parker: There are different answers to that. I am generally well treated. That is, I generally get reviews which are favorable. I've had enough negative ones to know the difference, but by and large, in ten years of publishing fiction I've been treated kindly by reviewers, which may be because I deserve to be. That aside, I think that I don't pay much attention to reviews. I don't read them. What was it Hemingway said? If you believe the good stuff they say, you gotta believe the bad too. In truth, I do not read the reviews. Dell sends them to me, and I throw them away without reading them. This is not to say if someone called me up and said that there was a feature piece on me in *Time* magazine I might not whip out and look at it. But generally I don't. They are of no value to me because

I am doing the best I can. If they say I should do something better, they may be right; but I can't. I'm doing it as well as I can. I never learned anything from a review that was useful to me. Reviews are normally for the furtherance of reviewers' careers. I've done a few reviews, and that's why I did them. I didn't do them for the thirty-five dollars someone was paying. All told it seems to me that if you get reviewed on a very large scale, say nationally or internationally, everything that can be said about you gets said. Plots are weak, characters are strong; strong character, weak plots. It's up to you. Trying to guide yourself by reading the reviews, you'd simply fragment. So I find that reviews are for readers, not for writers. I don't read them and consequently don't have a vigorous opinion about how they deal with my work.

NBMQ: What happened to the short story, particularly the mystery short story? Hard-boiled mystery fiction was born in the stories in *Black Mask*. Now it's difficult to find a good detective short story. Is it just a matter of markets?

Parker: I think so. It's hard to make a living writing short stories. There's damn few markets for them. One reason you don't find them is because *Dime Detective* and *Black Mask* are gone. I think a lot of the people who were writing short stories might be writing episodes for weekly television series now, and making a lot more money at it. Many of the detective series that you see on television—which I also don't watch, so I can't name them—are probably the equivalent to some extent of what would have been in *Black Mask* in the twenties and thirties and forties and up to the fifties, actually. I myself don't do short fiction because I have no skill at it. I wrote one at the behest of *Playboy* magazine; Alice Turner insisted. I said No; I really have no skill at short stories. She insisted that I try one anyway. They would give me lots of money and let me dance with a bunny. So I sent one in and they rejected it, thus proving my point.

NBMQ: Did you get to dance with a bunny?

Parker: No. Nothing. Zip. The bunny would have been the kill fee, but no. Then there are all the economic and practical reasons not to write stories. One novel will earn a lot more money than, say, five short stories.

NBMQ: Is *The Catskill Eagle* a novel-in-progress, or is it finished?

Parker: It will be out in June. I've finished it. I'm starting to noodle a new one.

NBMQ: It has been called the "Fat Spenser." Four hundred pages by contract. Why 400 pages?

Parker: Publishers like big books. Ninety to 100,000 words is what the contract said, I think it will probably come out in print to about 300 pages. But in my final typescript it was 422. A big book, from the publisher's point of view, is a more marketable book, and it achieves a different audience. It gets a different treatment; it is sold differently by the sales force. The size of the book, from this point of view, makes it strictly a "giant economy tube." That's why they wanted it large. I thought it would be interesting to try.

6

NBMQ: Is this an attempt to break out of the classifications we were talking about earlier?

Parker: Oh, sure. There's every reason to do that marketing-wise. To some extent, I have already broken out. *Valediction* was on the *Times* best-seller list for two consecutive weeks. Thank God for that second week, I have broken out in the way John D. MacDonald did, though not yet as vigorously, and sort of the way Elmore Leonard is in the process of doing, and the way Ross Macdonald did. If you are writing detective fiction, the good news is that it is easier to publish. What was it Chandler said? The average detective novel is no worse than the average straight novel, but the average straight novel won't get published. Detective novels are genre books, and it is easier to get them published because you can count on a minimum number of sales. There are people who will buy practically every new mystery that comes out, regardless. A publisher can give you a small advance and bring it out and make a small profit without much effort. The bad news is that if you are strictly a category detective writer there tends to be ceiling as well. I don't know what that ceiling is; it changes—12,000 copies, something like that. The big book tends to help a writer break out. If you are going to make an unduly successful living you have to break out of that mold—or write a hell of a lot of books, like Ed McBain, who has become an institution.

NBMQ: Spenser has now had twelve adventures (the same number of adventures as in the *Faerie*

Queene, by the way). Do you see any danger of Spenser becoming fat or less interesting to you?

Parker: No. It's what I do. I will periodically write a non-Spenser novel simply because now and then there are things that I choose to write about that are not appropriate to write about through his eyes, *Love and Glory* being the most recent example. I wanted a thirty-year love story, and there is no way you can have a thirty-year love story in a Spenser novel. But if I am remembered fondly by literary historians it will be for Spenser. It's what I do and I would want to do it regardless of whether I needed money, regardless of whether I made the front page of *The New York Times Book Review.* It is what I know how to do and what I do best. I have no interest in discontinuing it. I won't stop. No matter what you say I'm going to keep right at it.

NBMQ: Do you miss teaching?

Parker: No. Oh, God, no. I was no Mr. Chips. I went into it simply to find a job that would not require me to put in long hours so that I could write. I did that, got the Ph.D., and found myself teaching nine hours a week, which left a few hours open. I taught so I could write. Once I was able to make a living writing, I stopped teaching. Some people say I stopped teaching a long time before I left.

NBMQ: *Promised Land* is being made into a TV movie. Who is playing Spenser?

Parker: Actually there is a reception this evening by the governor to welcome the cast and crew before they start shooting. It is starring Robert Urich, who played

8

on "Vegas." And that's the only casting we have firmly made. The screenplay is by producer John Wilder and me. He did most of it. I did one revision. I have some title in this process—creative consultant, associate producer, or whatever—which means I can hang around and offer opinions. It's scheduled to be shot between now and February 5. I hope we get more people in the cast by then. I sat in a little on the casting. It's scheduled to run this spring or next fall or next spring on ABC. But if we don't deliver it in time for this spring, it will go on later. It will be a two-hour movie. There may be a series out of it. Nobody's calling this a pilot, but if it does well and ABC likes it— we have already started to work on the first four episodes of the series.

NBMQ: Are you worried about being spoiled by the glitter of network television?

Parker: No. Fear not. I think it is inappropriate for me to bite the hand that is at this moment feeding me, but you needn't fear that I will be seduced by network TV.

Promised Land

ROBERT B. PARKER

Promised Land (1976) marks a significant development in Robert Parker's skill as a novelist. Spenser takes on added dimension as a character and the complexity of his moral judgment is developed more fully than ever before. Two key characters of Parker's novels—Spenser's lover, Susan Silverman, and his strongarm friend, Hawk—are given their first full treatment in Promised Land, *amplifying the reader's understanding of Spenser himself. In the excerpt reprinted here, Susan meets Hawk for the first time and realizes the bond between him and Spenser.*

Robert Parker's comments on Promised Land, *written at the request of NBMQ, follow this excerpt.*

AFTER LUNCH we took coffee on the terrace by the pool, sitting at a little white table made of curlicued iron covered by a blue and white umbrella. It was mostly kids in the pool, splashing and yelling while their mothers rubbed oil on their legs. Susan Silverman was sipping coffee from a cup she held with both hands and looking past me. I saw her eyes widen behind her lavender sunglasses and I turned and there was Hawk.

He said, "Spenser."

I said, "Hawk."

He said, "Mind if I join you?"

I said, "Have a seat. Susan, this is Hawk. Hawk, this is Susan Silverman."

Hawk smiled at her and she said, "Hello, Hawk."

Hawk pulled a chair around from the next table, and sat with us. Behind him was a big guy with a sunburned face and an Oriental dragon tattooed on the inside of his left forearm. As Hawk pulled his chair over he nodded at the next table and the tattooed man sat down at it. "That's Powell," Hawk said. Powell didn't say anything. He just sat with his arms folded and stared at us.

"Coffee?" I said to Hawk.

He nodded. "Make it iced coffee though." I gestured to the waitress, ordered Hawk his iced coffee.

"Hawk," I said, "you gotta overcome this impulse toward anonymity you've got. I mean why not start to dress so people will notice you instead of always fading into the background like you do."

"I'm just a retiring guy, Spenser, just my nature." He stressed the first syllable in retiring. "Don't see no reason to be a clotheshorse." Hawk was wearing white Puma track shoes with a black slash on them. White linen slacks, and a matching white linen vest with no shirt. Powell was more conservatively dressed in a maroon-and-yellow-striped tank top and maroon slacks.

The waitress brought Hawk his iced coffee. "You and Susan having a vacation down here?"

"Yep."

"Sure is nice, isn't it? Always like the Cape. Got atmosphere you don't usually find. You know? Hard to define it, but it's a kind of leisure spirit. Don't you think, Spenser?"

"Yeah, leisure spirit. That what brought you down here, Hawk?"

"Oh, something like that. Had a chance to get in what you might call a working vacation. How 'bout yourself? Doing a little work for Harv Shepard?"

"I'll tell you if you'll tell me."

"Susan," Hawk said, "this man is a straight-ahead man, you know? Just puts it right out front, hell of a quality, I'd say."

Susan smiled at him and nodded. He smiled back.

"Come on, Hawk, knock off the Goody Two-shoes shtick. You want to know what I'm doing with Shepard and I want to know what you're doing with Shepard."

"Actually, it's a little more than that, babe, or a little less, whichever way you look at it. It ain't that I so much care what you're doing with Shepard as it is I want you to stop doing it."

"Ah-ha," I said. "A threat. That explains why you brought Eric the Red along. You knew Susan was with me and you didn't want to be outnumbered."

Powell said from his table, "What did you call me?"

Hawk smiled. "Still got that agile mind, Spenser."

Powell said again, "What did you call me?"

"It is hard, Powell," I said to him, "to look tough when your nose is peeling. Why not try some Sun Ban, excellent, greaseless, filters out the harmful ultraviolet rays."

Powell stood up. "Don't smart-mouth me, man. You wising off at me?"

"That a picture of your mom you got tattooed on your left arm?" I said.

He looked down at the dragon tattoo on his forearm for a minute and then back at me. His face got redder and he said, "You wise bastard. I'm going to straighten you out right now."

Hawk said, "Powell, I wouldn't if I was you."

"I don't have to take a lot of shit from a guy like this," Powell said.

"Don't swear in front of the lady," Hawk said. "You gotta take about whatever he gives you 'cause you can't handle him."

"He don't look so tough to me," Powell said. He was standing and people around the pool were beginning to look.

"That's 'cause you are stupid, Powell," Hawk said. "He is tough, he may be damn near as tough as me. But you want to try him, go ahead."

Powell reached down and grabbed me by the shirt front. Susan Silverman inhaled sharply.

Hawk said, "Don't kill him, Spenser, he runs errands for me."

Powell yanked me out of the chair. I went with the yank and hit him in the Adam's apple with my forearm. He said something like "ark" and let go of my shirt front and stepped back. I hit him with two left hooks, the second one with a lot of shoulder turned into it, and Powell fell over backward into the pool. Hawk was grinning as I turned toward him.

"The hayshakers are all the same, aren't they," he said. "Just don't seem to know the difference between amateurs and professionals." He shook his head. "That's a good lady you got there though." He nodded at Susan, who was on her feet holding a beer bottle she'd apparently picked up off another table.

Hawk got up and walked to the pool and dragged Powell out of it negligently, with one hand, as if the dead weight of a 200-pound man were no more than a flounder.

The silence around the pool was heavy. The kids were still hanging on to the edge of the pool, staring at us. Hawk said, "Come on, let's walk out to my car and talk." He let Powell slump to the ground by the table and strolled back in through the lobby. Susan and I went with him. As we passed the desk we saw the manager come out of his office and hurry toward the terrace.

I said, "Why don't you go down the room, Suze. I'll be along in a minute. Hawk just wants me to give him some pointers on poolside fighting." The tip of her tongue was stuck out through her closed mouth and she was obviously biting on it. "Don't bite your tongue," I said. "Save some for me." She shook her head.

"I'll stay with you," she said.

Hawk opened the door on the passenger's side of the Cadillac. "My pleasure," he said to Susan. If Hawk and I were going to fight he wouldn't pick a convertible for the place. I got in after Susan. Hawk went around and got in the driver's side. He pushed a button and the roof went up smoothly. He started the engine and turned on the air conditioning. A blue and white Barnstable Township police car pulled into the parking lot and two cops got out and walked into the motel.

Hawk said, "Let's ride around." I nodded and he put us in gear and slipped out of the parking lot.

"Where the hell did you get him?" I said to Hawk as we drove.

"Powell? Oh, man, I don't know. He's a local dude. People that hired me told me to work with him."

"They trying to set up an apprentice program?"

Hawk shrugged. "Beats me, baby, he got a long way to go though, don't he."

"It bother you that the cops are going to ask him what he was doing fighting with a tourist, and who the tourist was and who was the black stud in the funny outfit?"

Hawk shook his head. "He won't say nothing. He dumb, but he ain't that dumb."

Between us on the front seat Susan Silverman said, "What are we doing?"

Hawk laughed. "A fair question, Susan. What in hell are we doing?"

"Let me see if I can guess," I said. "I guess that Harv Shepard owes money to a man, probably King

Powers, and Hawk has been asked to collect it. Or maybe just oversee the disbursement of funds, whatever, and that things are going the way they should." I said to Susan, "Hawk does this stuff, quite well. And then surprise, I appear, and I'm working for Shepard. And Hawk and his employer, probably King Powers, wonder if Harv hired me to counteract Hawk. So Hawk has dropped by to inquire about my relationship with Harv Shepard, and to urge me to sever that relationship."

The Caddie went almost soundless along the Mid-Cape Highway, down Cape, toward Provincetown. I said, "How close, Hawk?"

He shrugged. "I have explained to the people that employ me about how you are. I don't expect to frighten you away, and I don't expect to bribe you, but my employer would like to compensate you for any loss if you were to withdraw from the case."

"Hawk," I said. "All this time I've known you I never could figure out why sometimes you talk like an account exec from Merrill Lynch and sometimes you talk like Br'er Bear."

"Ah is the product of a ghetto education." He pronounced both t's in ghetto. "Sometimes my heritage keep popping up."

"Lawdy me, yes," I said. "What part of the ghetto you living in now?"

Hawk grinned at Susan. "Beacon Hill," he said. He U-turned the Caddie over the center strip and headed back up Cape toward Hyannis. "Anyway, I told the people you weren't gonna do what they wanted, whatever I said, but they give me money to talk to you, so I'm talking. What your interest in Shepard?"

"He hired me to look for his wife."

"That all?"

"That's all."

"You find her?"

"Yes."

"Where?"

"I won't say."

"Don't matter, Shepard'll tell me. If I need to know."

"No." I shook my head. "He doesn't know either."

"You won't tell him?"

"Nope."

"Why not, man. That's what you hired on for."

"She doesn't want to be found."

Hawk shook his head again. "You complicate your life, Spenser. You think about things too much."

"That's one of the things that makes me not you, Hawk."

"Maybe," Hawk said, "and maybe you a lot more like me than you want to say. 'Cept you ain't as good looking."

"Yeah, but I dress better."

Hawk snorted, "Shit. Excuse me, Susan. Anyway, my problem now is whether I believe you. It sounds right. Sounds just about your speed, Spenser. Course you ain't just fell off the sugar-beet truck going through town, and if you was lying it would sound good. You still work for Shepard?"

"No, he canned me. He says he's going to sue me."

17

"Ah wouldn't worry all that much about the suing," Hawk said. "Harv's kinda busy."

"Is it Powers?" I said.

"Maybe it is, maybe it ain't. You gonna stay out of this, Spenser?"

"Maybe I will, maybe I won't."

Hawk nodded. We drove a way in silence.

"Who's King Powers?" Susan said.

"A thief," I said. "Loan sharking, numbers, prostitution, laundromats, motels, trucking, produce, Boston, Brockton, Fall River, New Bedford."

Hawk said, "Not Brockton anymore. Angie Degamo has got Brockton now."

"Angie chase Powers out?"

"Naw, some kind of business deal. I wasn't in it."

"Anyway," I said to Susan, "Powers is like that."

"And you work for him," she said to Hawk.

"Some."

"Hawk's a free-lance," I said. "But Powers asks him early when he's got Hawk's kind of work."

"And what is Hawk's kind of work?" Susan said, still to Hawk.

"He does muscle and gun work."

"Ah prefer the term soldier of fortune, honey," Hawk said to me.

"Doesn't it bother you," Susan said, "to hurt people for money?"

"No more than it does him." Hawk nodded to me.

"I don't think he does it for money," she said.

"Tha's why Ah'm bopping down the Cape in a new

Eldorado and he's driving that eight-year-old hog with the gray tape on the upholstery."

"But . . ." Susan looked for the right words. "But he does what he must, his aim is to help. Yours is to hurt."

"Not right," Hawk said. "Maybe he aiming to help. But he also like the work. You know? I mean he could be a social worker if he just want to help. I get nothing out of hurting people. Sometimes just happens that way. Just don't be so sure me and old Spenser are so damn different, Susan."

We pulled back into the parking lot at the motel. The blue and white was gone. I said, "You people through discussing me yet, I got a couple things to say, but I don't want to interrupt. The subject is so god-damned fascinating."

Susan just shook her head.

"Okay," I said. "This is straight, Hawk. I'm not working for Shepard, or anybody, at the moment. But I can't go home and let you and Powers do what you want. I'm gonna hang around, I think, and see if I can get you off Shepard's back."

Hawk looked at me without expression. "That's what I told them," he said. "I told them that's what you'd say if I came around and talked. But they paying the money. I'll tell them I was right. I don't think it gonna scare them."

"I didn't suppose it would," I said.

I opened the door and got out and held it open for Susan. She slid out, and then leaned back in and spoke to Hawk. "Goodby," she said. "I'm not sure what to

say. Glad to have met you wouldn't do, exactly. But"
—she shrugged—"thanks for the ride."

Hawk smiled at her. "My pleasure, Susan. Maybe I'll see you again."

I closed the door and Hawk slid the car out of the parking lot, soundless and smooth, like a shark cruising in still water.

Commentary on
Promised Land

ROBERT B. PARKER

Promised Land, from which this excerpt came, is the first book in which Hawk appears. As I was writing *Promised Land*, it was not my conscious intention to make him a recurring character. He seemed merely a suitable antagonist for Spenser when I began. It is one of the cliches of the word business to say that a character takes over an author, or in some way acts as if he (or she) had a life of his (or her—liberation do get clumsy) own. This is, of course, tripe. As I have better reason to know than anyone, Hawk is a figment of my imagination and has no existence outside of it. No character does; to believe otherwise is to believe in some sort of literary voodoo. What did happen, however, is that Hawk offered a lot of artistic opportunity.

Hawk is, and the racial pun is intended, the dark side of Spenser. He is what Spenser might have been had he grown up black in a white culture. The hero of books like mine is often outside of the culture. It could be argued, and I'd be willing to so argue, that the hero of most American books is poised, if not in opposition to the official culture, at least in counterbalance to it. If such a hero is non-white, his poise will be more radically asocial, because his exclusion will be more complete. While Spenser is both in and out of the culture, Hawk displays no such uncertainty. His presence in the books provides me an opportunity to examine some aspects of the American Myth, and to comment, sometimes directly, sometimes obliquely, on racism.

These things and several others occurred to me, not so much as I was writing *Promised Land*, but next time out, when I was working on *The Judas Goat* and had occasion to call Hawk back. I'm glad they did occur to me. Hawk in his containment and invulnerability adds substance and ulteriority to the work. Like Susan, his presence helps define Spenser and enlarge our ability to think about the issues Spenser engages. Like Susan, he is interesting in himself and interesting in the context he provides.

The Ripoff

JIM THOMPSON

"Thompson is my particular admiration among 'original' authors," novelist R. V. Cassill has declared. "The Killer Inside Me (1952) is exactly what French enthusiasts for existential American violence were looking for in the works of Dashiell Hammett, Horace McCoy and Raymond Chandler. None of these men ever wrote a book within miles of Thompson's." Jim Thompson published twenty-nine novels between 1942 and 1973, all but one of which were paperback originals. His devout circle of admirers claim he wrote psychological thrillers unequaled in post-war American fiction.

Cassill has written that "Thompson at his best hits notes that are stunningly convincing. Not his materials, but the reckless play of his imagination in the moral debris gives one pause. In his hands the writing instrument sounds the trilling of genuine American demons."

Thompson had revised the typescript for The Ripoff, *but he died in 1977 before he could arrange publication. This installment is the first of four.*

1

I DIDN'T HEAR HER until she was actually inside the room, locking the door shut behind her. Because that kind of place, the better type of that kind of place—and this *was* the better type—has its tap roots in quiet. Anonymity. So whatever is required for it is provided: thick walls, thick rugs, well-oiled hardware. Whatever is required, but no more. No bath, only a sink firmly anchored to the wall. No easy chairs, since you are not there to sit. No radio or television, since the most glorious of diversions is in yourself. Your two selves.

She was scowling agitatedly, literally dancing from foot to foot, as she flung off her clothes, tossing them onto the single wooden chair where mine were draped.

I laughed and sat up. "Have to pee?" I said. "Why do you always hold in until you're about to wet your pants?"

"I don't always! Just when I'm meeting you, and I don't want to take time to—*oops! Whoops!* Help me, darn it!" she said, trying to boost herself up on the sink. "*Hall-up!*"

I helped her, holding her on her porcelain perch until she had finished. Then I carried her to the bed, and lowered her to it. Looked wonderingly at the tiny immensity, the breathtaking miracle of her body.

She wasn't quite five feet tall. She weighed no more than ninety-five pounds, and I could almost encompass her waist with one hand. But somehow there was no skimpiness about her. Somehow her flesh flowed and curved and burgeoned. Extravagantly, deliciously lush.

"Manny," I said softly, marveling. For as often as I had seen this miracle, it remained new to me. "Manuela Aloe."

"Present," she said. "Now, come to bed, you good-looking, darlin' son-of-a-bitch."

"You know something, Manny, my love? If I threw away your tits and your ass, God forbid, there wouldn't be anything left."

Her eyes flashed. Her hand darted and swung, slapping me smartly on the cheek.

"Don't you talk that way to me! Not ever!"

"What the hell?" I said. "You talk pretty rough yourself."

She didn't say anything. Simply stared at me, her eyes steady and unblinking. Telling me, without telling me, that how she talked had no bearing on how I should talk.

I lay down with her, kissed her, and held the kiss. And suddenly her arms tightened convulsively, and I was drawn onto and into her. And then there was a fierce muted sobbing, a delirious exulting, a frantic hysterical whispering. . . .

"*Oh, you dirty darling bastard! You sweet son-of-a-bitch! You dearest preciousest mother-loving sugar-pie. . . .*"

Manny.

Manuela Aloe.

I wondered how I could love her so deeply, and be so much afraid of her. So downright terrified.

And I damned well knew why.

After a while, and after we had rested a while, she placed her hands against my chest and pushed me upward so that she could look into my face.

"That was good, Britt," she said. "Really wonderful. I've never enjoyed anything so much."

"Manny," I said. "You have just said the finest, the most exciting thing a woman can say to a man."

"I've never said it to anyone else. But, of course, there's never been anyone else."

"Except your husband, you mean."

"I never said it to him. You don't lie to people about things like this."

I shifted my gaze, afraid of the guilt she might read in my eyes. She laughed softly, on a submerged note of teasing.

"It bothers you, doesn't it, Britt? The fact that there was a man before you."

"Don't be silly. A girl like you would just about have to have other men in her life."

"Not *men*. Only the one man, my husband."

"Well, it doesn't bother me. He doesn't, I mean. Uh, just how did he die, anyway?"

"Suddenly," she said. "Very suddenly. Let me up now, will you please?"

I helped her to use the sink, and then I used it. It couldn't have taken more than a minute or two, but when I turned around she had finished dressing. I was startled, although I shouldn't have been. She had the quick, sure movements characteristic of so many small women. Acting and reacting with lightning-like swiftness. Getting things done while I was still thinking about them.

"Running off mad?" I said, and then, comprehending, or thinking that I did, "Well, don't fall in, honey. I've got some plans for you."

She frowned at me reprovingly, and still playing it light, I said she couldn't be going to take a bath. I'd swear she didn't need a bath, and who would know better than I?

That got me another frown, so I knocked off the kidding. "I like your dress, Manny. Paris job, is it?"

"Dallas. Neiman-Marcus."

"Tsk, tsk, such extravagance," I said. "And you were right there in Italy, anyway, to pick up your shoes."

She laughed, relenting. "Close, but no cigar," she said, pirouetting in the tiny, spike-heeled pumps. "I. Pinna. You like?"

"Like. Come here, and I'll show you how much."

"Gotta go now, but just wait," she said, sliding me a sultry glance. "And leave the door unlocked. You'll have some company very soon."

I said I wondered who the company could be, and she said archly that I should just wait and see; I'd really be surprised. Then she was gone, down the hall to the bathroom, I supposed. And I stretched out on the bed, pulling the sheet up over me, and waited for her to return.

The door was not only unlocked, but ever-so-slightly ajar. But that was all right, no problem in a place like this. The lurking terror sank deeper and deeper into my mind, and disappeared. I yawned luxuriously, and closed my eyes. Apparently I dozed, for I suddenly sat up to glance at my wristwatch. Automatically obeying a whispered command which had penetrated my subconscious. "*Watch.*"

I said I sat up.

That's wrong.

I only started to, had barely lifted my head from the pillows, when there was a short snarling-growl. A threat and a warning, as unmistakable as it was deadly. And slowly, ever so slowly, I sank back on the bed.

There was a softer growl, a kind of gruff whimper. Approval. I lay perfectly still for a time, scarcely breathing—and it is easy to stop breathing when one is scared stiff. Then, without moving my head, I slanted my eyes to the side. Directly into the unblinking stare of a huge German Shepherd.

His massive snout was only inches from my face. The grayish-black lips were curled back from his teeth. And I remember thinking peevishly that he had too many, that no dog could possibly have this many teeth. Our eyes met and held for a moment. But dogs, members of the wolf family, regard such an encounter as a challenge. And a rising growl jerked my gaze back to the ceiling.

There was that gruff whimper again. Approval. Then, nothing.

Nothing but the wild beating of my heart. That, and the dog's warm breath on my face as he stood poised so close to me. Ready to move—decisively—if I should move.

"*Watch!*" He had been given an order. And until that order was revoked, he would stay where he was. Which would force me to stay where I was . . . lying very, very still. As, of course, I would not be able to do much longer.

Any moment now, I would start yawning. Accumulated tension would force me to. At almost any moment my legs would jerk, an involuntary and uncontrollable reaction to prolonged inactivity. And when that happened. . . .

The dog growled again. Differently from any of his previous growls. With the sound was another, the brief thud-thud of a tail against the carpet.

A friend—or perhaps an acquaintance—had come into the room. I was afraid to move my head, as the intruder was obviously aware, so she came around to the foot of the bed where I could see her without moving.

It was the mulatto slattern who sat behind the desk in the dimly lit lobby. The manager of the place, I had always assumed. The mock concern on her face didn't quite conceal her malicious grin; there was spiteful laughter in her nominally servile voice.

"Well, jus' looky heah, now! Mistah Britton Rainstar with a doggy in his room! How you doin', Mistah High-an'-mighty Rainstar?"

"G-goddamn you—!" I choked with fear and fury. "Get that dog out of here! Call him off!"

She said, "Shuh, man." She wasn't tellin' *that* dog to do nothin'. "Ain't my houn'. Wouldn't pay no attention to me, 'ceptin' maybe to bite my fat ass."

"But goddamn it—! I'm sorry," I said. "Please forgive me for being rude. If you'll get Manny—Miss Aloe, please. Tell her I'm very sorry, and I'm sure I can straighten everything out if she'll just—just—"

She broke in with another "Shuh" of disdain. "Where I get Miss Manny, anyways? Ain't seen Miss Manny since you-all come in t'day."

"I think she's in the bathroom, the one on this floor. She's got to be here somewhere. Now, please—!"

"Huh-*uh*! Sure ain't callin' her out of no bathroom. Not me, no, sir! Miss Manny wouldn't like that a-tall!"

"B-but—" I hesitated helplessly. "Call the police then. *Please!* And for God's sake, hurry!"

"Call the p'lice? *Here?* Not a chance, Mistah Rainstar. No, siree! Miss Manny sho' wouldn't like that!"

"To hell with what she likes! What's it to you, anyway? Why, goddamn it to hell—"

"Jus' plenty t'me what she likes. Miss Manny my boss. That's right, Mistah Rainstar." She beamed at me falsely. "Miss Manny bought this place right after you-all started comin' here. Reckon she liked it real well."

She was lying. She had to be lying.

She wasn't lying.

She laughed softly, and turned to go. "You lookin' kinda peak-id, Mistah Rainstar. Reckon I better let you get some rest."

"Don't," I begged. "Don't do this to me. If you can't do anything else, at least stay with me. I can't move, and I can't lie still any longer, and—and that dog will kill me! He's trained to kill! S-so—so—please—" I gulped, swallowing an incipient sob, blinking the tears from my eyes. "Stay with me. Please stay until Miss Manny comes back."

My eyes cleared.

The woman was gone. Moved out of my line of vision. I started to turn my head, and the dog warned me to desist. Then, from somewhere near the door, the woman spoke again.

"Just stay until Miss Manny come back? That's what you said, Mistah Rainstar?"

"Yes, please. Just until then."

"But what if she don' come back? What about that, Mistah Rainstar?"

An ugly laugh, then. A laugh of mean merriment. And then she was gone. Closing the door firmly this time.

And locking it.

2

The terror had begun three months before.

It began at three o'clock in the morning with Mrs. Olmstead shaking me into wakefulness.

Mrs. Olmstead is my housekeeper, insofar as I have one. An old age pensioner, she occupies a downstairs bedroom in what, in better times, was called the Rainstar Mansion. She does little else but occupy it, very little in the way of housekeeping. But, fortunately, I require little, and necessarily pay little. So one hand washes the other.

She wasn't a very bright woman at best, and she was far from her best at three in the morning. But I gathered from her babbling and gesturing that there was an emergency somewhere below, so I pulled on some clothes over my pajamas and hurried downstairs.

A Mr. Jason was waiting for me, a stout apoplectic-looking man who was dressed pretty much as I was. He snapped out that he just couldn't have this sort of thing, y'know. It was a goddamn imposition, and I had a hell of a lot of guts giving out his phone number. And so forth and so on.

"Now, look," I said, finally managing to break in on him. "Listen to me. I didn't give out your number to anyone. I don't know what the hell it is, for Christ's sake, and I don't want to know. And I don't know what you're talking about."

"Yeah? Y'don't, huh?" He seemed somewhat mollified. "Well. Better hurry up. Fellow said it was an emergency; matter of life and death."

He lived in an elaborate summer home about three miles from mine, in an area that was still very good. He stopped his car under the porte-cochere, and preceded me into the entrance hall; then withdrew a few feet while I picked up the telephone.

I couldn't think who would be making a call to me under such circumstances. There just *wasn't* anyone. No one at the Foundation would do it. Except for the check which they sent me monthly, I had virtually no contact with the Hemisphere Foundation. As for Constance, my wife, now a resident, an apparently permanent one, at her father's home in the midwest. . . .

Constance had no reason to call. Except for being maimed and crippled, Constance was in quite good health. She would doubtless die in bed . . . thirty or forty years from now . . . sweetly smiling her forgiveness for the accident I had caused.

So she would not call, and her father would not. Conversation with me was something he did his best to avoid. Oh, he had been scrupulously fair, far more than I would have been in his place. He had publicly exonerated me of blame, stoutly maintaining to the authorities that there was no real evidence pointing to my culpability. But without saying so, he had let me know that he would be just as happy without my company or conversation.

So . . . ?

"Yes?" I spoke into the phone. "Britton Rainstar, here."

"Rainstar"—a husky semi-whisper, a disguised voice. "Get this, you deadbeat fuck-off. Pay up or you'll die cryin'. Pay up or else."

"*Huh!* Wh-aat?" I almost dropped the phone. "What—who is this?"

"I kid you not, Rainstar. Decorate the deck, or you'll be trailing turds from here to Texas."

I was still sputtering when the wire went dead.

Jason glanced at me, and looked away. "Bet you could use a drink. Always helps at a time like this."

"Thanks, but I guess not," I said. "If you'll be kind enough to drive me home. . . ."

He did so, mumbling vague words of sympathy (for just what, he didn't know). At my house, with its crumbling veranda and untended lawn, he pressed a fifty-dollar bill into my hand.

"Get your phone reconnected, okay? No, I insist! And I'm sorry things are so bad for you. Damned shame."

I thanked him humbly, assuring him that I would do as he said.

By the time Mrs. Olmstead arose and began preparing breakfast, I had had two more callers, both crankily sympathetic as, like Jason, they brought word of a dire emergency.

I went with them, of course. How could I refuse? Or explain? And what if there actually *was* an emergency? There was always a chance, a million-to-one chance, that my caller might have a message of compelling importance. So it was simply impossible— impossible for me, at least—to ignore the summons.

The result was the same each time. An abusive demand to pay up or to suffer the ugly consequences.

I accepted some weak, lukewarm coffee from Mrs. Olmstead; I even ate a piece of her incredible toast and a bite or two of the scrambled eggs she prepared, which, preposterous as it seems, were half-raw but overcooked.

Ignoring Mrs. Olmstead's inquiries about my "emergency" calls, I went up to my room and surrendered to a few hours of troubled rest. I came back downstairs shortly after noon, advised Mrs. Olmstead that I would fix my own lunch and that she should do as she pleased. She trudged down the road to the bus stop, going I knew not where nor cared. I cleaned myself up and dressed, not knowing what I was going to do, either. And not caring much.

From the not-too-distant distance came a steady rumbling and clattering and rattling; the to-and-fro passage of an an almost unbroken parade of trucks.

Through the many gabled windows, their shutters opened to the spring breeze, came the sickishly-pungent perfume of what the trucks were carrying.

I laughed. Softly, sadly, wonderingly. I jumped up, slamming a fist into my palm. I sat back down and got up again. Aimlessly left the room to wander aimlessly through the house. Through the library with its thread-bare carpet and its long, virtually empty bookshelves. Through the lofty drawing room, its faded tapestry peeling in tatters from the walls. The grand ballroom, its parquet floor declining imperceptibly but ominously with the vast weight of a rust-ruined pipe-organ.

I came out onto the rear veranda, where glass from shattered windows splattered over the few unsalable items of furniture that remained. Expensive stained glass, bright with color.

I stood looking off into that previously mentioned, not-too-distant distance. It was coming closer; it had come quite a bit closer since yesterday, it seemed to me. And why not, anyway, as rapidly as those trucks were dumping their burden?

At present, I was merely—*merely!*—in the environs of a garbage dump. But soon it would be right up to my back door. Soon, I would be right in the middle of the stinking, rat-infested horror.

And maybe that was as it should be, hmm? What better place for the unwanted, unneeded, and worthless?

Jesus! I closed my eyes, shivering.

I went back through the house and up to my bedroom. I glanced at myself in a full-length mirror, and

I doubt that I looked as bad as my warped and splotched reflection. But still I cursed and groaned out loud.

I flung off my clothes and showered vigorously. I shaved again, doing it right instead of half-assed. And then I began rummaging through my closets, digging far back in them and uncovering items I had forgotten.

An hour later, after some work with Mrs. Olmstead's steam iron, some shoe polish, and a buffing brush, I again looked at myself. And warped as it was, the mirror told me my efforts were well spent indeed.

The handmade shoes were eternally new, ever magnificent, despite their age. The cambric shirt from Sulka and the watered-silk Countess Mara tie *were* new—long-ago Christmas presents which I had only glanced at and returned to their gift box. And a decade had been wonderfully kind to the Bond Street suit, swinging full circle through fads and bringing it back in style again.

I frowned, studying my hair.

The shagginess was not too bad, not unacceptable, but a trim was certainly in order. The gray temples and the gray streak down the center were also okay, a distinguished contrast for the jet blackness. However that yellowish tinge that gray hair shittily acquires was *not* all right. I needed to see a truly good hair man, a stylist, not the barber-college cruds that I customarily went to.

I examined my wallet—twelve dollars plus the fifty Jason had given me. So I *could* properly finish the job I had started, hair and all. And the wonders it would do for my frazzled morale to look decent again, the way Britton Rainstar had to look . . . having so little else but looks.

But if I did that, if I didn't make at least a token payment to Amicable Finance—!

The phone rang. It had not been disconnected, as Jason had assumed. Calling me at other numbers was simply part of the "treatment."

I picked up the phone and identified myself.

A cheery man's voice said that he was Mr. Bradley, Amicable comptroller. "You have quite a large balance with us, Mr. Rainstar. I assume you'll be dropping in today to settle up?"

I started to say that I was sorry, that I simply couldn't pay the entire amount, as much as I desired to. *"But I'll pay something; that's a promise, Mr. Bradley. And I'll have the rest within a week—I swear I will! J-just don't do anything. D-don't hurt me. Please, Mr. Bradley."*

"Yes, Mr. Rainstar? What time can I expect you in today?"

"You can't," I said.

"How's that?" His voice cracked like a whip.

"Not today or any other day. You took my car. I repaid your loan in full, and you still took my car. Now—"

"Late charges, Rainstar. Interest penalties. Repossession costs. Nothing more than your contract called for."

I told him he could go fuck for what the contract

37

called for. He could blow it out his ass. "And if you bastards pull any more crap on me, any more of this calling me to the phone in the middle of the night. . . ."

"Call you to the phone?" *He was laughing at me.* "Fake emergency calls? What makes you think we were responsible?"

I told him why I thought it; why I knew it. Because only Amicable Finance was lousy enough to pull such tricks. Others might pimp for their sisters at a nickel a throw, but they weren't up to Amicable's stunts.

"So here's some advice for you, you liver-lipped ass-hole! You fuck with me any more, and it'll be shit in the fan! Before I'm through with you, you'll think lightning struck a crapper. . . !"

I continued a minute or two longer, growing more elaborate in my cursing. And, not surprisingly, I had quite a vocabulary of curses. Nothing is sacred to children, just as anything unusual is an affront to them, a challenge which cannot be ignored. And when you have a name like Britton Rainstar, you are accepted only after much fighting and cursing.

I slammed down the phone. Frightened stiff by what I had done, yet somehow pleased with myself. I had struck back for a change. For once in a very long time, I had faced up to the ominous instead of ignoring or running from it.

I fixed the one drink I had in the house, a large drink of vodka. Sipping it, feeling the dullness go out of my heart, I decided that I *would* by god get the needful done with my hair. I would look like a man, by god, not the Jolly Green Giant, when Amicable Finance started giving me hell.

Before I could weaken and change my mind, I made an appointment with a hair stylist. Then I finished my drink, dragging it out as long as I could, and stood up.

And the phone rang.

I almost didn't answer it; certain that it would get me nothing but a bad time. But few men are strong enough to ignore a ringing telephone and I am not one of them.

A booming, infectiously good-natured voice blasted into my ear.

"Mr. Rainstar, Britt? How the hell are you, kid?"

I said I was fine, and how the hell was he? He said he was just as fine as I was, laughing uproariously. And I found myself smiling in spite of myself.

"This is Pat Aloe, Britt. Patrick Xavier Aloe, if you're going to be fussy." Another roar of laughter. "Look, kid. I'd come out there, but I'm tied up tighter than a popcorn fart. So's how about you dropping by my office in about an hour? Well, two hours, then."

"But—well, why?" I said. "Why do you want to see me, Mr.—uh, Pat?"

"Because I owe you, Britt, baby. Want to make it up to you for those pissants at Amicable. Don't know what's the matter with the stupid bastards, anyway."

"But . . . Amicable?" I hesitated. "You have something to do with them?"

A final roar of laughter. Apparently, I had said something hilariously funny. Then, good humor flooding

me, but I also wanted to see him, even though I didn't
his voice, he declared that he not only wanted to see
know it yet. Thus, the vote for seeing each other was
unanimous by his account.

"So how about it, Britt, baby? See you in a couple
of hours, okay?"

"Who am I to buck a majority vote?" I said. "I'll
see you, Pat, uh, baby."

3

I got out of the cab at a downtown office building. I
entered its travertine marble lobby and studied the
large office directory affixed to one wall. It was glassed
in, a long oblong of white plastic lettering against a
black felt background. The top line read:

PXA HOLDING CORPORATION

Beneath it, in substantially smaller letters, were the
names of sixteen companies, including that of Amicable Finance. The final listing, in small red letters,
read:

P.X. Aloe

—P. H.

M. Francesca Aloe

'Allo, Aloe, I thought, stepping into the elevator.
Patrick Xavier, M. Francesa, and Britt, baby, makes
three. Or something. But whereof and why, for god's
sake?

I punched the button marked P.H., and was zoomed

forty floors upward to the Penthouse floor. As I debarked into its richly furnished reception area, a muscular young man with gleaming black hair stepped in front of me. He looked sharply into my face, then smiled and stepped back.

"How are you, Mr. Rainstar? Nice day."

"How are you?" I said, for I am nothing if not polite. "A nice day so far, at least."

A truly beautiful, beautifully-dressed woman came forward, and urgently squeezed my hand.

"Such a pleasure to meet you, Mr. Rainstar! Do come with me, please."

I followed her across a hundred feet or so of carpet (a foot deep or so) to an unmarked door. She started to knock, then jerked her hand back. Turned to me still smiling, but rather whitishly.

"If you'll wait just a moment, please. . . ."

She started to shoo me away, then froze at the sound from within the room. A sound that could only be made by a palm swung against a face. Swung hard, again, again. . . . Like the stuttering, staccato crackling of an automatic rifle.

It went on for all of a minute, a very long time to get slapped. Abruptly, as though a gag had been removed, a woman screamed.

"N-no! D-don't, please! I'll never do—!"

The scream ended with the suddenness of its beginning. The slapping also. The beautiful, beautifully dressed young woman waited about ten seconds. (I counted them off silently.) Then she knocked on the door and ushered me inside.

41

"Miss Manuela Aloe," she said. "Mr. Britton Rainstar."

A young woman came toward me smiling; rubbing her hand, her *right* hand, against her dress before extending it to me. "Thank you, Sydney," she said, dismissing the receptionist with a nod. "Mr. Rainstar, let's just sit here on the lounge."

We sat down on the long velour lounge. She crossed one leg over the other, rested an elbow on her knee, and looked at me smiling, her chin propped in the palm of her hand. I looked at her—the silver-blond hair, the startlingly black eyes and lashes, the flawlessly creamy complexion. I looked and found it impossible to believe that such a delicious bonbon of a girl would do harm to anyone.

Couldn't I have heard a recording? And if there had been another woman, where was she? The only door in the room was the one I had entered by, and no one had passed me on the way out.

"You look just like him," Manuela was saying. "We-ell, almost just. You don't have your hair in braids."

I said, "What?" And then I said, "Oh," for several questions in my mind had been answered. "You mean Chief Britton Rainstar," I said. "The Remington portrait of him in the Metropolitan."

She said no, she'd missed that one, darn it. "I was talking about the one in the Royal Museum by James MacNeill Whistler. But tell me. Isn't Britton a kind of funny name for an Indian chief?"

"Hilarious," I said. "I guess we got it from the nutty

whites the Rainstars intermarried with, early and often. Now, if you want a real honest-to-Hannah, jumpin'-by-Jesus Indian name—well, how does George strike you?"

"George?" she laughed. "*George?*"

"George Creekmore. Inventor of the Cherokee alphabet, and publisher of the first newspaper west of the Mississippi."

"And I guess that'll teach me," she smiled, coloring slightly. "But anyway, you certainly bear a strong resemblance to the Chief. Of course, I'd heard that all the Rainstar men did, but—"

"We're hard to tell apart," I agreed. "The only significant difference is in the pockets of later generations."

"The pockets?"

"They're empty," I said, and tapped myself on the chest. "Meet Lo, the poor Indian."

"Hi, Lo," she said, laughing. And I said, "Hi," and then we were silent for a time.

But it was not an uncomfortable silence. We smiled and looked at each other without self-consciousness, both of us liking what we saw. When she spoke it was to ask more questions about the Rainstar family; and while I didn't mind talking about it, having little else to be proud of, there were things I wanted to know, too. So, after rambling on a while I got down to them.

"Like when and why the heck," I said, "am I seeing P.X. Aloe?"

"I don't think you'll be able to see Uncle Pat today," she said. "Some last-minute business came up. But

43

there's nothing sinister afoot"—she gave me a reassuring little pat on the arm. "Now, unless you're in a hurry. . . ."

"Well, I *am* due in Washington to address the cabinet," I said. "I thought it was already addressed, but I guess someone left off the zone number."

"You dear!" she laughed delightedly. "You absolute dear! Let's go have some drinks and dinner, and talk and talk and talk. . . ."

She got her hat and purse from a mahogany cabinet. The hat was a sailor with a turned-up brim, and she cocked it over one eye, giving me an impish look. Then she grinned and righted it, and the last faint traces of apprehension washed out of my mind.

Give another woman a vicious slapping? This darling, diminutive child? Rainstar, you are nuts!

We took the elevator down to PXA's executive dining room, in a sub-basement of the building. A smiling maitre d' with a large menu under his arm came out of the shadows and bowed to us graciously.

"A pleasure to see you, Miss Aloe. And you, too, sir, needless to say."

"Not at all," I said. "*My* pleasure."

He looked at me a little startled. I am inclined to gag it up and talk too much when I am uneasy or unsure of myself, which means that I am almost always gagging it up and talking too much.

"This is Mr. Britton Rainstar, Albert (Albehr)," Manuela Aloe said. "I hope you'll be seeing him often."

44

"My own hope. Will you have a drink at the bar while your table is being readied?"

She said we would, and we did. In fact, we had a couple, since the night employees were just arriving at this early hour, and there was some delay in preparing our table.

"Very nice," I said, taking an icy sip of martini. "A very nice place, Miss Aloe. Or is it Mrs.?"

She said it was Miss—she had taken her own name after her husband died—and I could call her Manny if I liked. "But yes—" she glanced around casually— "it is nice, isn't it? Not that it shouldn't be, considering."

"Uh-huh," I said. "Or should I say ah-ha? I'm afraid I'm going to have to rush right off to Geneva, Manny."

"Wha-aat?"

"Just as soon as I pay for these drinks. Unless you insist on going dutch on them."

"Silly!" She wriggled deliciously. "You're with me, and everything's complimentary."

"But you said considering," I pointed out. "A word hinting at the dread unknown, in my case at least. To wit, money."

"Oh, well," she shrugged, dismissing the subject. "Money isn't everything."

4

With an operation as large and multifaceted as PXA, one with so many employees and interests, it was impossible to maintain supervision and surveillance in every place it might be required. It would have been impossible, even if PXA's activities were all utterly legitimate instead of borderline, with personnel who figuratively cried out to be spied upon. Pat Aloe had handed the problem to his niece Manny, a graduate student in psychology. After months of consultation with behaviorists and recording experts, she had come up with the bugging system used throughout the PXA complex.

It was activated by *tones* and was uncannily accurate in deciding when a person's voice tone was not what it should be. Thus Bradley, the man who had called me this morning, had been revealed as a "switcher," one who diverted business to competitors. So all of his calls were completely recorded, instead of sporadically spotchecked.

"I see," I nodded to Manny, as we dawdled over coffee and liqueurs, "about as clearly as I see through mud. Everything is completely opaque to me."

"Oh, now, why do you say that?" she said. "I'd seen that portrait when I was a little girl, and I'd never gotten it out of my mind. So when I found out that the last of the Rainstars was right here in town. . . !"

"Recalling part of the conversation," I said, "you must have felt that the last of the Rainstars needed his mouth washed out with soap."

She laughed and said nope, cursing out Bradley had been a plus. "That was just about the clincher for you with Pat. Someone of impeccable background and breeding, who could still get tough if he had to."

"Manny," I said, "exactly what is this all about, anyway? Why PXA's interest in me?"

"Well. . . ."

"Before you answer, maybe I'd better set you straight on something. I've never been mixed up in anything shady, and PXA seems to be mixed up in nothing else but. Oh, I know you're not doing anything illegal, nothing you can go to prison for. But still, well—"

"PXA is right out in the open," Manny said firmly. "Anyone that wants to try can take a crack at us. We don't rewrite any laws, and we don't ask any to be written for us. We don't own any big politicians. I'd say that for every dollar we make with our so-called shady operations, there's a thousand being stolen by some highly respectable cartel."

"Well," I nodded uncomfortably, "there's no disputing that, of course. But I don't feel that one wrong justifies another, if you'll pardon an unpardonable cliche."

"Pardoned." She grinned at me openly. "We don't try to justify it. No justifications, no apologies."

"And this bugging business." I shook my head. "It seems like something right out of *Nineteen Eighty-Four*. It's sneaky and Big Brotherish, and it scares the hell out of me."

Manny shrugged, remarking that it was probably everything I said. But bugging wasn't an invention of PXA, and it didn't and wouldn't affect me. "We're on your side, Britt. We're against the people who've been against your people."

47

"My people?" I said, and I grimaced a little wryly. "I doubt that any of us can be bracketed so neatly anymore. We may be more of one race than we are another, but I suspect we're all a little of everything. White, yellow, black, and red."

"Oh, well—" she glanced at her wristwatch. "You're saying that there are no minorities?"

I said that I wasn't sure what I was saying, or, rather, what the point to it was. "But I don't believe that a man who's being pushed around has a right to push anyone but the person pushing him . . . if you can untangle that. His license to push is particular, not general. If he starts lashing out at everyone and anyone, he's asking for it, and he ought to get it."

It was all very high-sounding and noble, and it also had the virtue, fortunately or otherwise, of being what I believed. What I had been bred to believe. And now I was sorry I had said it. For I seemed to be hopelessly out of step with the only world I had, and again I was about to be left alone and afraid in that world, which I had had no hand in making. This lovely child, Manny, the one person to be kind to me or show interest in me for so very long, was getting ready to leave.

She was looking at me, brows raised quizzically. She was patting her mouth with her napkin, then crumpling it to the table. She was glancing at herself in the mirror in the purse. Then snapping the purse shut and starting to rise.

And then, praise be, glory to the Great Mixed Blood Father, she sat back down.

"All right," she said crisply. "Let's say that PXA is interested in using the Rainstar name. Let's say that. It would be pretty stupid of us to dirty up that name, now, wouldn't it?"

"Well, yes, I suppose it would," I said. "And look. I'm sorry if I said anything to offend you. I always kid around and talk a lot whenever I'm—"

"Forget it. How old are you?"

"Thirty-six."

"You're forty. Or so you stated on your loan application. What do you do for a living, if you can call it that?"

I said why ask me something she already knew? "That information's also on the application. Along with practically everything else about me, except the number and location of my dimples."

"You mean you have some I can't see?" She smlied, her voice friendlier, almost tender. "But what I meant to ask was, what do you write for this Hemisphere Foundation?"

"Studies. In-depth monographs on this region from various aspects: ecological, etiological, ethological, ethnological. That sort of thing. Sometimes one of them is published in Hemisphere's *Quarterly Reports*. But they usually go in the file-and-forget department."

"Mmm-hmm," she said thoughtfully, musingly. "Very interesting. I think something could be worked out there. Something satisfactory to both of us."

"If you could tell me just what you have in mind. . . ."

"Well, I'll have to clear it with Pat, of course, but. . . . Thirty-five thousand a year?"

49

"That's not what I meant. I—*what?*" I gasped. "Did you say *thirty-five thousand?*"

"Plus expenses and certain fringe benefits."

"Thirty-five thousand," I said, running a finger around my collar. "Uh, how much change do you want back?"

She threw back her head and laughed, hugging herself ecstatically. "Ah, Britt, Britt," she said, brushing mirth tears from her eyes. "Everything's going to be wonderful for you. I'll make it wonderful, you funny-sweet man. Now, do me a small favor, hmm?"

"Practically anything," I said, "if you'll laugh like that again."

"Please don't worry about silly things, like our bugging system. Everyone knows we have it. We're out in the open on that as we are with everything else. If someone thinks he can beat it, well, it isn't as if he hadn't been warned, is it?"

"I see what you mean," I said, although I actually didn't. I was just being agreeable. "What happens when someone is caught pulling a fast one?"

"Well, naturally," she said, "we have to remove him from the payroll."

"I see," I said again. Lying again when I said it. Because, of course, there are many ways to remove a man from the payroll. (Horizontal was one that occurred to me.) My immediate concern, however, as it so often is, was me. Specifically, the details of my employment. But I was not allowed to inquire into them.

Before I could frame another question, she had

moved with a kind of unhurried haste, with the quick little movements which typified her. Rising from her chair, tucking her purse under her arm, gesturing me back when I also started to rise; all in one swift-smooth, uninterrupted action.

"Stay where you are, Britt," she smiled. "Have a drink or something. I'll have someone pick you up and drive you home."

"Well. . . ." I settled back into my chair. "Shall I call you tomorrow?"

"I'll call you. Pat or I will. Good-night, now."

She left the table, her tinily full figure with its crown of thick blond hair quickly losing itself in the dining room's dimness.

I waited. I had another liqueur and more coffee. And continued to wait. An hour passed. A waiter brushed by the table, and when he had gone, I saw a check lying in front of me.

I picked it up, a nervous lump clotting in my stomach. My eyes blurred, and I rubbed them, at last managing to read the total.

Sixty-three dollars and thirty cents.

Sixty-three dollars and—!

I don't know how you are in such situations, but I always feel guilty. The mere need to explain that such and such is a mistake, et cetera, stiffens my smile exaggeratedly and sets me to sweating profusely and causes my voice to go tremolish and shaky. So that I not only feel guilty as hell, but also look it.

It is really pretty terrible.

It is no wonder that I was suspected of the attempted

51

murder of my wife. The wonder is that I wasn't lynched.

Albert, the maitre d', approached. As I always do, I overexplained, apologizing when I should have demanded apologies. Sweating and shaking and squeakily stammering, and acting like nine kinds of a damned fool.

When I was completely self-demolished, Albert cut me off with a knifing gesture of his hand.

"No," he said coldly, "Miss Aloe did not introduce you to me. If she had, I would have remembered it." And he said, "No, she made no arrangement about the check. Obviously, the check is to be paid by you."

Then he leaned down and forward, resting his hands on the table, so that his face was only inches from mine. And I remember thinking that I had known this was going to happen, not exactly this, perhaps, but something that would clearly expose the vicious potential of PXA. A taste of what could happen if I incurred the Aloe displeasure.

For she had said—remember?—that they did not pretend or apologize. You were warned, you knew exactly what to expect *if.*

"You deadbeat bastard," Albert said. "Pay your check or we'll drag you back in the kitchen and beat the shit out of you."

5

I was on an aimless tour of the country when I met my wife-to-be, Connie. I'd gotten together some money through borrowing on or peddling off the few remaining Rainstar valuables, so I'd bought a car and taken off. No particular, no clear objective in mind. I simply didn't like it where I was, and I wanted to find a place where I would like it. Which, of course, was impossible. Because the reason I disliked places I was in— and the disheartening knowledge was growing on me —was my being in them. I disliked *me*—me, myself, and I, as kids used to say, and far and fast as I ran I could not escape the bastardly trio.

Late one afternoon, I strayed off the highway and wound up in a homey little town nestled among rolling green hills. I also wound up with a broken spring from a plunge into a deep rut, and a broken cylinder and corollary damage from getting out of the rut.

The town's only garage was the blacksmith shop. Or, to put it another way, the blacksmith did auto repairs . . . except for those who could drive a hundred-plus miles to the nearest city. The blacksmith-mechanic quoted a very reasonable price for repairing my car, but he would have to send away for parts, and what with one thing and another, he couldn't promise to have the work done in less than a week.

There was one small restaurant in the town, sharing space with the post office. But there was no hotel, motel or boarding house. The blacksmith-mechanic suggested that I check with the real estate dealer to see if some private family would take me in for a few days. Without much hope, I did so.

The sign on the window read *Luther Bannerman— Real Estate & Insurance*. Inside, a young woman was disinterestedly pecking away at an ancient typewriter with a three-row keyboard. She was a little on the scrawny side, with mouse-colored hair. But she laughed wildly when I asked if she was Luther Bannerman and otherwise endeared herself to me by her childish eagerness to be of help, smiling and bobbing her head sympathetically as I explained my situation. When I had finished, however, she seemed to draw back a bit, becoming cautiously reserved.

"Well, I just don't know, Mr.—Britton, is it?"

"Rainstar. Britt, for Britton, Rainstar."

"I was going to say, Mr.—oh, I'll make it Britt, okay? I was just going to say, Britt. We're kind of out of the mainstream here, and I'm afraid you'd find it hard to keep in touch and carry on your business affairs, and—" she bared her teeth in a smile—"and so forth and so on."

I explained that I had no pressing business affairs, not a single so forth, let alone a so on. I was just traveling, seeing the country and gathering material for a book. I also explained, when she raised the question of accommodations for my wife and family, that I had none with me or elsewhere and that my needs were solely for myself.

At this she insisted on pouring me coffee from the pot on a one-burner heater. Then, having made me "comfy"—also nauseated: the coffee was lousy—she hurried back to a small partitioned-off private office. After several minutes of closed-door conversation, she returned with her father, Luther Bannerman.

Of course he and she collectively insisted that I stay at their house. (It would be no trouble at all, but I could pay a little something if I wanted to.)

Of course I accepted their invitation. And, of course, I was in her pants the very first night. Or, rather, I was in what was in her pants. Or, to be absolutely accurate, she was in my pants. She charged into my room as soon as the light went out. And I did not resist her, despite her considerable resistability.

I felt that it was the very least I could do for her, although quite a few others had obviously done as much. I doubt that they had fought for it either, since it simply wasn't the sort of thing for which men do battle. Frankly, if it had been tendered as inspiration for the launching of a thousand ships (or even a toy canoe), not a one would have hoisted anchor.

Ah, well. Who am I to kid around about poor Connie and her over-stretched snatch? Or to kid about anyone, for that matter? It is one of Fate's saddest pranks to imbue the least sexually appetizing of us with the hugest sexual appetitites. To atone for that joke, I feel, is the obligation of all who are better endowed. And in keeping that obligation I have had many sorrier screws than Connie. I have received little gratitude for my efforts. On the contrary, I invariably wind up with a worse fucking than the fucking I got. For it is also one of Fate's jokes to dower superiority complexes on girls with the worst fornicating furniture. And they seem to feel justified in figuratively giving you something as bad as they have given you literally.

Of course Connie's father discovered us in coitus before the week was out. And, of course, I agreed to do the "right thing" by his little girl, which characteristically was the easiest thing for me to do. Or so it seemed at the time. I may struggle a bit, but I almost always do the easiest thing. Or what seems to be and never is.

At the time I was born, promising was the word for Rainstar prospects. Thus I was placed on the path of least resistance early in life, and I remained on it despite my growing awareness that promise was not synonymous with delivery. I had gathered too much speed to get off, and I could find no better path to be on anyway. I'm sure you've seen people like me.

If I stumbled over an occasional rock I might curse and kick out at it. But only briefly, and not very often at all. I was so unused to having my course unimpeded that normally I fell apart when it was. It was the only recourse for a man made defenseless by breeding and habit.

Both Connie and her father were provoked to find that my prosperousness was exactly one hundred percent more apparent than real. They whined that I had deceived them, maintaining that since I was nothing but a well-dressed personable bum, I should have said so. Which, to me, seemed unreasonable. After all, why do your utmost *not* to look like a bum if you are going to announce that you are one?

Obviously, there were basic philosophical differences between me and the Bannermans. But they finally seemed resigned to me, if not to my way of thinking.

In fact, I was given their rather grim assurance that I would come around to their viewpoint eventually and be much the better man for it. Meanwhile, Mr. Bannerman would not only provide me with a job, but would give Connie and me $100,000 life insurance policies as a wedding present.

I felt that it was money wasted since Connie, like all noxious growths, had a built-in resistance to scourge, and I had grown skilled in the art of self-preservation, having devoted a lifetime to it. However, it was Mr. Bannerman's money, and I doubted that it would amount to much, since he was in the insurance business as well as real estate.

So he wrote the policies on Connie and me, with each of us the beneficiary of the other. Connie's policy was approved. Mine was rejected. Not on grounds of health, my father-in-law advised me. My health was excellent for a man wholly unaddicted to healthful hard work.

The reason for my rejection was not spelled out to Mr. Bannerman, but he had a pretty good idea as to its nature, and so did I. It was a matter of character. A man with a decidedly truncated work history—me that is—who played around whenever he had the money for playing around—again me—was apt to come to an early end, and possibly a bad one. Or so statistics indicated. And the insurance company was not betting a potential $100,000—$200,000, double indemnity—on my longevity when their own statistics branded me a no-no.

With unusual generosity, Mr. Bannerman conceded

that there were probably a great many decadent bums in the world, and that I was no worse than the worst of them. The best course for me was to reapply for the policy, after I had "proved myself" with a few years of steady and diligent employment.

To this end, he hired me as a commission salesman. It proved nothing except what I already knew—that I was no more qualified to sell than I apparently was for any other gainful occupation.

I continued to be nagged by Papa and Daughter Bannerman, but was given up on after a few weeks. Grimly allowed to "play around" with my typewriter while they—"other people"—*worked* for a living. Neither would hear of a divorce, nor the suggestion that I get the hell out of their lives. I was to "come to my senses" and "be a man"—or do *something*. Surely, I could do *something!*

Well, though, the fact was I couldn't do something. The something that I could do did not count as something with them. And they were keeping the score.

Thus matters stood at the time of the accident which left me unscathed but almost killed Connie. I, an unemployed bum living on my father-in-law's bounty, was driving the car when the accident happened. And while I carried no insurance, my wife was heavily insured in my favor.

"Dig this character." Albert, the maitre d', jerked a thumb at me, addressing the circle on onlooking diners. "These bums are getting fancier every day, but

*this one takes the brass ring. What did you say your
name was, bum?"*

"Rainstar."

*A reassuring hand dropped on my shoulder. "He
said it was, and I say it is. Any other questions?"*

"Oh—certainly not, sir! A stupid mistake on my
part, sir, and I'm sure that—"

"Come on, Britt. Let's get out of here."

6

We stood waiting for the elevator, Albert and I and
my friend, whoever he was. Albert was begging, seem-
ing almost on the point of tears.

". . . a terrible mistake, believe me, gentlemen! I
can't think how I could have been guilty of it. I recall
Mr. Rainstar perfectly now. Everything was exactly as
he says, but—"

"But it slipped your mind. You completely forgot."

"Exactly!"

"So you treated me like any other deadbeat. You
were just following orders."

"Then you do understand, sir?"

"I understand," I said.

We took the elevator up to the street, my friend and
I. I accompanied him to his car, trying to remember
who he was, knowing that I had had far more than a
passing acquaintance with him at one time. At last, as
we passed under a streetlight, it came to me.

"Mr. Claggett, Jeff Claggett!" I wrung his hand. "How could I ever have forgotten?"

"Oh, well, it's been a long time." He grinned deprecatingly. "You're looking good, Britt."

"Not exactly a barometer of my true condition," I said. "But how about you? Still with the university?"

"Police Department, detective sergeant." He nodded toward the lighted window of a nearby restaurant. "Let's have some coffee and a talk."

He was in his early sixties, a graying, square-shouldered man with startlingly blue eyes. He had been chief of campus security when my father was on the university faculty. "I left shortly after your dad did," he said. "The coldblooded way they dumped him was a little more than I could stomach."

"It wasn't very nice," I admitted. "But what else could they do, Jeff? You know how he was drinking there at the last. You were always having to bring him home."

"I wish I could have done more. I would have drunk more than he did, if I'd had his problems."

"But he brought them all on himself," I pointed out. "He was slandered, sure. But if he'd just ignored it, instead of trying to get the UnAmerican Activities Committee abolished, it would all have been forgotten. As it was, well, what's the use talking?"

"Not much," Claggett said. "Not anymore."

I said, "Oh, for God's sake." It sounded like I was knocking the old man, and, of course, I didn't mean to. "I didn't mind his drinking, per se. It was just that it left him vulnerable to being kicked around by people who weren't fit to wipe his ass."

Jeff Claggett nodded, saying that a lot of nominally good people seemed to have a crappy streak in them. "Give them any sort of excuse, and they trot it out. Yeah, and they're virtuous as all hell about it. So-and-so drinks, so that cleans the slate. They don't even owe him common decency."

He put down his coffee cup with a bang and signalled for a refill. He sipped from it, sighed, and grimaced tiredly.

"Well, no use hashing over the past, I guess. How come you were in that place I got you out of tonight, Britt?"

"Through a misunderstanding," I said firmly. "A mistake that isn't going to be repeated."

"Yeah?" He waited a moment. "Well, you're smart to steer clear of 'em. We haven't been able to hang anything on them, but, by God, we will."

"With my blessings," I said. "You were on official business tonight?"

"Sort of. Just letting them know we were on the job. Well—" He glanced at his watch, and started to rise. "Guess I better run. Can I drop you some place?"

I declined with thanks, saying that I had a little business to take care of. He said, "Well, in that case. . . ."

"By the way, I drove past the old Rainstar place a while back, Britt. Looks like someone is still living there."

"Yes," I said. "I guess someone is."

"In a *dump?* The city garbage dump? But—" His voice trailed away, comprehension slowly dawning in his eyes. Finally, he said, "Hang around a minute, Britt. I've got to make a few phone calls, and then we'll have a good talk."

We sat in Claggett's car, in the driveway of the Rainstar Mansion, and he frowned in the darkness, looking at me curiously. "I don't see how they can do this to you, Britt. Grab your property while you're out of the state."

"Well, they paid me for it," I said. "Around three thousand dollars after the bank loan was paid. And they gave me the privilege of staying in the house as long as I want to."

"Oh, shit!" Claggett snorted angrily. "How long is that going to be? You've been swindled, Britt, but you sure as hell don't have to hold still for it!"

"I don't know," I said. "I don't see that there's much I can do about it."

"Of course there's something you can do! This place was deeded tax-free to the Rainstars in perpetuity, in recognition of the thousands of acres the family had given to the state. It's not subject to mortgage or the laws of eminent domain. Why, I'll tell you, Britt, you go into court with this deal, and. . . ."

I listened to him without really listening. There was nothing he could tell me that I hadn't told myself. I'd argued it all out with myself, visualizing the newspaper stories, the courtroom scenes, the endless questions. And I'd said to hell with it. I knew myself, and I knew I couldn't do it for any amount of money.

"I can't do it, Jeff," I cut in on him at last. "I don't want to go into the details, but I have a wife in another state. An invalided wife. I was suspected of trying to kill her. I didn't, of course, but—"

"Of course you didn't!" Jeff said warmly. "Murder just isn't in you. Anyway, you wouldn't be here if there was any real case against you."

"The case is still open," I said. "I'm not so sure I'm in the clear yet. At any rate, the story would be bound to come out if I made waves over this condemnation deal, so I'm not making any. I, the family and I, have had nothing but trouble as far back as I remember. I don't want any more."

"No one wants trouble, damn it," Claggett scowled. "But you don't avoid it by turning your back on it. The more you run from, the more you have chasing you."

"I'm sure you're right," I said. "But just the same. . . ."

"Your father would fight, Britt. He *did* fight! They didn't get away with piling garbage on him!"

"They didn't?" I said. "Well, well."

We said good-night.

He drove off, gravel spinning angrily from the wheels of his car.

I entered the house, catching up the phone on its first ring. I said hello, putting a lot of ice into the word.

I started to say a lot more, believing that the caller was Manuela Aloe, but fortunately I didn't. Fortunately, since the call was from Connie, my wife.

"Britt? Where have you been?"

"Out trying to make some money," I said. "I wasn't successful, but I'm still trying."

She said that she certainly hoped so. All her terrible expenses were awfully hard on her daddy, and it did seem like a grown, healthy man like me, with a good education, should be able to do a little something. "If you could just send me a *little* money, Britt. Just a teensy-weensy bit—"

"Goddamn it!" I yelled. "What's with this teensy-weensy crap? I send you practically everything I get from the Foundation, and you know I do because you wrote them and found out how much they pay me! You had to embarrass me, like a goddamned two-bit shyster!"

She began to cry. She said it wasn't her fault that she was crippled, and that she was worried out of her mind about money. I should just be in the fix she was in for a while, and see how I liked it. And so forth and so on, ad infinitum, ad nauseum.

And I apologized and apologized and apologized. And I swore that I would somehow someway get more money to her than I had been sending. And then I apologized three or four hundred additional times, and at last, when I was hoarse from apologies and promises, she wished me sweet dreams and hung up.

Sweet dreams!

I was so soaked with sweat that you would have thought I'd had a wet dream.

Which was not the kind of dream one had about Connie.

7

Mrs. Olmstead set breakfast before me the next morning, remarking—doubtless by way of whetting my appetite—that we would probably have rat shit in the food before long.

"I seen some chasin' around the backyard yesterday, so they'll be in the house next. Can't be this close to a garbage dump without havin' rats.'

"I see," I said absently. "Well, we'll face the problem when it comes."

'Time t'face it is now," she asserted. "Be too late when the rats is facin' us."

I closed my ears to her gabbling, finishing what little breakfast I was able to eat. As I left the table, Mrs. Olmstead handed me a letter to mail when I went to town, if I didn't mind, o' course.

"But I was going to work at home today," I said. "I hadn't really planned on going to town."

"How come you're all fixed up, then?" she demanded. "You don't never fix yourself up unless you're going somewhere."

I promised to mail the letter, if and when. I tucked it into my pocket as I went into the living room, noting that it was addressed to the old age pension bureau.

More than a year ago her monthly check had been three dollars short—by her calculations, that is. She had been writing them ever since, sometimes three times a week, demanding reimbursement. I had pointed out that she had spent far more than three dollars in postage, but she stubbornly persisted.

Without any notion of actually working, I went into the small room, a one-time serving pantry which does duty as my study. I sat down at my typewriter, wrote a few exercise sentences and various versions of my name. After about thirty minutes of such fiddling around, I jumped up and fled to my bedroom. Fretfully examined myself in the warped full-length mirror.

And I thought: All dressed up and no place to go. There would be no call from PXA. If there was one, I couldn't respond to it. Not after the ordeal I had been put through last night. No one who was serious about giving me worthwhile employment would have done such a thing to me. And it must have been done deliberately. An outfit as cruelly efficient as PXA didn't allow things like that to come about accidentally.

I closed my eyes and clenched my mind to the incident, unable to live through it again even in memory. Wondered why it was that I seemed constantly called upon to face things I couldn't. I went back down to my whilom study, but not to my typewriter. What was there to write? Who would want anything written by me?

I sat down on a small love seat. A spiny tuft of horsehair burst through the upholstery and stabbed me in the butt, something that seemed to typify the hilarious tragedy of my life. I was pining away of a broken heart or something, but instead of being allowed a little dignity and gravity, I got my ass tickled.

Determinedly, I stayed where I was and as I was. Bent forward with my head in my hands. Sourly resisting the urge to squirm or snicker.

Poor Lo. . . .

"Poor Lo. . . ."

I chuckled wryly, poking fun at myself.

"Well, screw it," I said. "They may kill me, but they can't eat me."

There was a light patter of applause. Hand clapping.

I sat up, startled, and Manuela Aloe laughed and sat down at my side.

"I'm sorry," she said. "I spoke to you a couple of times, but you didn't hear me."

"B-but—but—" I began to get hold of myself. "What are you doing here?"

"Your housekeeper showed me in. I came out here because I was afraid you wouldn't come to the office after the terrible time you must have had last night."

"You were right," I said. "I wouldn't have gone down to your office. And there really wasn't much point to your coming out here."

"I did send a car to pick you up last night, Britt. I don't blame you for being angry, but I did send it."

"Whatever you say," I said.

"I don't know what happened to the driver. No one's seen him since. Our people aren't ordinarily so irresponsible, but it's not unheard of. But anyway, I am sorry."

"So much for the driver," I said. "Now what about Albert?"

"Albert," she grimaced. "I don't know whether it was booze or dope or just plain stupidity that made him do what he did. I don't care, either. He's out of a job as of this morning, and he'll be a long time in getting another one."

She nodded to me earnestly, the dark eyes warm with concern. I hesitated, wanting to swallow my pride —how could I afford pride? Remembering Connie's demands for money.

"There was something else," I said. "Something that came to me when I was outside your office yesterday."

"Yes?" She smiled encouragingly. "What was that, Britt?"

I hesitated again, trying to find some amiable euphemisms for what was virtually an accusation. And finding excuses instead. After all, her office *would* logically have sound equipment in it; devices for auditing the tapes. And why, when I was so strongly drawn to this girl, and when I needed money so badly, should I continue to squeeze her for apologies and explanations?

"Yes, Britt?"

"Nothing," I said. "No, I mean it. Thinking it over, I seem to have found the answer to my own question."

That wasn't true. Aside from the woman's being slapped, there was something else. The fact that PXA had milked me for all kinds of personal information as a condition for granting my loan. My likes and dis-

68

likes, my habits and weaknesses. Information that could be used to drive me up a figurative wall, should they take the notion.

But I meant to give them no cause to take such a notion. And I am an incurable optimist, always hoping for the best despite the many times I have gotten the worst.

Manny was studying me, her dark eyes boring into mine. Seemingly boring into my mind. A sudden shadow blighted the room, and I was chilled with a sickening sense of premonition.

Then she laughed gaily, gave herself a little shake, and assumed a business-like manner.

"Well, now," she said briskly. "I've had a long talk with Uncle Pat, and he's left everything to me. So how about a series of pamphlets on the kind of subjects you deal with for the Foundation?"

"It sounds fine," I said. "Just—well—fine."

"The pamphlets will be distributed free to schools, libraries, and other institutions. They won't carry any advertising. Just a line to the effect that they are sponsored by PXA as a public service."

I said that was fine, too. Just fine. She opened her blond leather purse, took out a check and handed it to me. A check for $3,500. Approximately $2,900 for the first month's work, with the rest for expenses.

"Well?" She looked at me pertly. "All right? Any questions?"

I let out a deep breath. "My God!" I breathed fervently. "Of course it's all right! And no, no questions."

She smiled and stood up, a lushly diminutive figure

in her fawn-colored panstsuit. Her breasts and her bottom bulged deliciously against the material; seemed to strain for release. And I thought thoughts that brought a flush to my face.

"Come on." She wiggled her fingers. "Show me around, hmm? I've heard so much about this place, I'm dying to see it."

"I'm afraid it's not much to see anymore," I said. "But if you're really interested in ruins. . . ."

I showed her through the house, or much of it. She murmured appreciatively over the decaying evidence of past grandeur, and regretfully at the ravages of time.

When we finished out tour of the house Manny again became business-like. "We'll have a lot of conferring to do to get this project operating, Britt. Do you want an office, or will you work here?"

"Here, if it's agreeable to you," I said. "I have a great deal of research material here, and I'm used to the place. Of course if it's inconvenient for you. . . ."

"Oh, we'll work it out," she promised. "Now, if you'll drive me back to town. . . ."

The car she had driven out in was mine, she explained, pointing to the gleaming new vehicle which stood in the driveway. Obviously I would need a car, and PXA owed me one. And she did hope I wouldn't be stuffy about it.

I said I never got stuffy over gifts of single cars. Only fleets of them, and not always then. Manny laughed and gave me a playful punch on the arm.

"Silly! Now, come on, will you? We have a lot to do today."

We did have a lot to do, as it turned out. At least we did a lot—far more than I anticipated. But that's getting ahead of the story. To take events in their proper order:

I drove into town, Manny sitting carelessly close to me. I deposited the check in my bank, drew some cash and returned to the car—*my* car. It was lunch time by then, so we lunched and talked. I talked mostly, since I have a knack for talk, if little else, and Manny seemed to enjoy listening to me.

We came out of the restaurant into mid-afternoon, and talking, I drove around until sunset. By which time, needless to say, we were ready for a drink. We had it, rather we had *them*, and eventually we had dinner. When twilight fell we were on the outskirts of town, parked by the lake which served as the reservoir for the city's water system.

Manny's legs were tucked up in the seat. Her head rested on my shoulder and my arm was around her. It was really a very nice way to be.

"Britt . . ." she murmured, breaking the drowsy, comfortable silence. "I've enjoyed myself so much today. I think it's been the very best day in my life."

"You're a thief, Manuela Aloe," I said. "You've stolen the very speech I was going to make."

"Tell me something, Britt. How does anyone as nice as you are, as attractive and intelligent and bubbling over with charm—how does he, why does he. . . ?"

'Wind up as I have?" I said. "Because I never found a seller's market for those things until I met you."

It was a pretty blunt thing to say. She sat up with a

start, glaring at me coldly. But I smiled at her determinedly and said I meant no offense.

"Let's face it, Manny. The Rainstar name isn't worth much anymore, and my talent never was. So the good looks and the charm, et cetera, is what I've sold, isn't it?"

"No it isn't!" she snapped, and then hesitating, biting her lip, "Well, not entirely. You wouldn't have gotten the job if you hadn't been like you are, but neither would you have gotten it if you hadn't been qualified."

"So it was half one, half the other," I said. "And what's wrong with fifty-fifty?"

"Nothing. And don't you act like there is, either!"

"Not even a little bit?"

"No!"

"All right, I won't," I said. "Providing you smile real pretty for me, and then lie down with your head in my lap."

She did so, although the smile was just a trifle weak. I bent down and kissed her gently, and was kissed in return. I put a hand on her breast, gave it a gentle squeeze. She shivered delicately, eyes clouding.

"I'm not an easy lay, Britt. I don't sleep around."

'What am I to do with you, Manny?" I said. "You are now twice a thief."

"I guess I've been waiting for you. It had to be someone like you, and there wasn't anyone like that until you."

"I know," I said. "I also have been waiting."

You can see why I said it, why I just about *had* to

say it. She was my munificent benefactor, she was gorgeous beyond my wildest dreams and she obviously wanted and needed to be screwed. So what the hell else could I do?

"Britt. . . ." She wiggled restlessly. "I have a live-in maid at my apartment."

"Unfortunate," I said. "My housekeeper also lives in."

"Well? Well, Britt dear?"

"Well, I know of a place. . . ." I broke off, carefully amended the statement. "I mean, I've *heard* of one. It's nothing fancy, I understand. No private baths or similar niceties. But it's clean and comfortable and safe. . . . Or so I'm reliably told."

"Well?" she said.

"Well?" I said.

She didn't say anything. Simply reached out and turned on the ignition.

Backfire

RAYMOND CHANDLER

Although Raymond Chandler's Hollywood career was frustrating, he was involved with important movies: Double Indemnity *(with Billy Wilder),* Strangers on a Train *(with Alfred Hitchcock), and* The Blue Dahlia, *made from his original screenplay. Sometime in 1946 or 1947, Chandler wrote this screen story on speculation, but no one was interested in hiring him to develop it into a screenplay. Published only as a collector's edition (Santa Barbara: Santa Teresa Press, 1984), "Backfire" is an example of the first step in the filmscript process, the "original story" that precedes the "treatment" in which plot and characters are developed before going on to the actual screenplay. As Robert B. Parker noted in his introduction to the edition in which this story appeared, George is an example of the Chandler attitude: ". . . a vision of chivalric possibility, of hope, maybe only the nostalgia, that honor and courage in the defense of goodness is sufficient to endure."*

GEORGE COMES HOME from the wars (I'm as sick of this as you are, I'm just spitballing) to find, say, his wife has been killed in an auto accident on a dark road in a fog at night, at a bad turn. He has no suspicions of foul play. (The cops had, but they didn't get anywhere, so clammed up.) George finds the small town drear and too full of memories now, and he moves on.

He remembers Edna, his wife, always talked of her childhood in Poonville, Oregon. George says that's as good as any. He goes on there and gets a job and rooming is tight, so he is introduced by Mary, a girl friend of Edna's, to Joe, a nice guy, also out of service, and they room together. They become pals. George has asked Mary not to tell anybody who he was or anything about his being married to Edna. He doesn't want talk or sympathy. He wants a new life in a new town, but it kind of helps his loneliness to think that Edna was a kid along these streets, and drank Cokes and ate ice cream in this drugstore, and went to this Bijou movie house, and waggled a little red and green flag over on the high school football field.

George is a nice guy, not simple, not bitter. Just lonely. Joe is a nice guy too, but his eyes are a little bitter and his mind is not so clean after the war. But the boys get on fine.

Joe finds out somehow who George is. And Joe is the boy who was stationed in Edna's town in the war and went off the track with her and killed her because she wanted too much of his life.

Joe thinks George came there to get him, that this friendly act is just an act. Joe thinks he is in love with Mary. George is, but doesn't know it yet. Mary is in love with Joe, who gets the women that way.

Little things begin to happen to George. Look funny. Almost got hurt that time. Then he does get hurt. Just misses being killed. Doesn't know it himself, but another guy puts him wise. "Somebody did that on purpose, George." George wonders, talks to Joe, Who the hell would want to hurt him? Joe thinks this is more act, kind of third degree. It's beginning to get him. He ought to move on. But Mary has dough and she can be had. Better marry her first and then move on.

But George is doing all right with Mary too. Joe knows damn well that he either gets them quick or not at all. George is a distance runner.

Then George gets a letter from a friend back home. "I guess you're all over Edna's death by now, George. And you've made nice friends and met a nice girl. Maybe I ought to go on keeping my mouth shut, but I don't like the way Edna got killed. Never did. I was talking to Beattie Lewis the other night, the cop who investigated it. Beattie never liked it either. He never liked the guy that was playing around with Edna while you were away, even if he was a soldier from the camp. The trouble is, Beattie says, this guy, Joe Westerman, wasn't even in town that night. He had leave in New York. But Beattie sure would have liked to been able to convince somebody this needed a little more work. Only the chief just couldn't give him the time."

Joe Westerman. That's the guy George is rooming with. In Poonville. Why in Poonville, of all the thousand small towns in the U.S.A. he could go to?

George asks him. Joe looks surprised. "My first camp," he says. "I had a pretty swell time here too. Only I didn't use all of my opportunities. Guy hates to think he didn't do that. Matter of fact, why are you here, George?"

76

"My wife was born here." "Wife? Never knew you had one." "She's dead. Auto accident." He lights a cigarette and blows smoke idly. "That is, they said it was an accident. But I just had a letter—oh, well, let's forget it, Joe. Guess I'll take a shower."

He does. Joe goes through his clothes. He doesn't find the letter. George sees him do it. Joe does not see George.

George goes to see Mary. Tells her he's going back home. There's something he wants to look into. "Would it make any difference to you whether I came back here, Mary?" Mary just looks at him. "Or will you be all right with Joe?" Mary flares up a bit. Then she busts out crying, "I—I guess I'm in love with Joe," she says. "I'm sorry, George. I guess that's how it is."

George says fine. "Always provided he's the right kind of guy for you." "Do you think I wouldn't know?" George: "I know *somebody* who didn't."

He leaves. Mary is not sore, but she is hurt. George starts to pack, tells Joe. Joe offers to drive him to the station. Fine. They just miss the train. Fine. Make it at the junction easy. Fine. Out in the country George says: "Stop a minute, Joe. Here's the letter you didn't find."

Joe reads it. "Yeah," he admits. "Edna and I were pals. I got to know her because she came from here and I was in camp here. Kind of a bond. After she was killed I wanted to come back. Kind of funny. We both came here for the same reason, you and I."

"But that isn't why you thought I came here, is it, Joe?" "Huh?" "Well, I have to make that train. Better get moving." Joe doesn't move. George tells him why he is going home. "But you see, Joe, I'm really doing it for *your* sake. Mary's in love with you. I've got to know." Joe: "Know what?" "I've got to know whether Edna's death was an accident—like the ones I had here. On account of Mary I've got to know. She's in love with you, Joe."

Joe: "And if it wasn't an accident?" George: "Then I have to find out where you were that night. If it's not too late to find out. How about driving on? Or would you rather pull that gun?"

Joe pulls the gun he has been holding in his pocket. "No bullets in it, Joe. I took them out." Joe smiles. "I reloaded it, sucker. Think I'd overlook that?" "There's something else I ought to tell you, Joe." "Save it, get under this wheel and drive."

They drive. They come to a bridge over the river. It's a swift river. Joe makes George stop. Get out. Down the bank with you. They go down the bank. Joe lectures on murder. "Saps kill twice the same way. Not me. By the time they find you, bud—and this is your car, remember?"

They go down to the edge of the river. Deep, fast, dark. "Stand on the bank, George. I don't like to do this, but a guy has to. Lucky you were leaving town tonight. Helps. So long, pal."

Joe lifts the gun and fires. There is an unnaturally heavy explosion. Well, who said what kind of gun it was.

Darkness. Something goes into the river. Steps.

There is a digging sound off. A car starts and fades off into the night.

A man gets on a train. A car is left in a garage.

They miss Joe around town after a while. Mary is silent. They miss George, too. Mary knows where he went, but she doesn't tell. She doesn't know where Joe went. They find George's car. And a guy took a ticket for New York. What did he look like? Looked like a guy with a suitcase looks. They go to Joe's room. Clothes not packed. Went standing up. George left nothing. Oh well, these ex-soldiers. They don't stay put.

Mary packs a suitcase herself. Her old man is bothered, but Mary's always known how to take care of herself.

Beattie Lewis is in the squad room, bored as hell. No business. A man wants to see him. The door opens. George walks in.

They bust Joe's alibi. They look up the coroner's report. The autopsy. Edna was thrown from the car, hit side of head against rock, neck broken, death instantaneous. George says: "How about the hyoid bone?" "Nothing." "You mean, you didn't look at it?" The coroner admits that. Cause of death obvious. George says: "Sure, blood, crushed skull, broken neck, all you wanted. But all that could be faked. How far was she thrown?" "Too damn far," Beattie says, "for my taste. And too clear. And the way the car was broke up she ought to of been trapped in it. But they happen all kinds of ways. You never know. I had one lying on the roof of a sedan once, dead as a pickled herring." "I'd like to know about the hyoid bone," George says. "Either that or a bruise on her chin." "Little late for that, son," the coroner says. "It might mean my own neck," George says. "You see, I killed the guy who did it."

They pinch George and then they get the doc that did the autopsy. "No signs of strangulation," he says. "No bruises on chin." He looks over his notes. "Only one thing you could even notice apart from the main injury. The woman was wearing an anklet and the anklet lock made a bruise on her leg. That could happen all sorts of ways." Beattie shakes his head. "Boy, am I dumb. That tells the whole story. Look, this guy knocks the woman out with a sandbag on the side of her head. Then he winds something strong but soft around her ankles and swings her the way an adagio dancer swings his partner. Then he slams her into the rock. Maybe twice. Let's see, did this guy ever—"

So they find out he did, before the war. He was in a cheap act with a girl and he swung her by the ankles shoulder high.

They find Joe down river. His head is in bad shape. Pieces of steel have torn off half his face and a lot of his throat and chest. Or maybe it was fishes.

Mary goes to see George in jail. "George, why did you run away? Why didn't you just tell your story?"

George: "Because what I did was murder—unless I could prove self-defense—unless I could prove that Joe had tried to kill me before. I could only prove that by proving a motive. The motive was that he killed Edna. So I had to prove he killed Edna. And I had to have time to do that, so I had to put him in the river. After all, it was his own idea. Suppose I said he held a gun on me and fired and the gun killed him. That's just me talking. Even if I got off, I was cooked with you. This way I've got what they call a cumulative defense."

They take George back to Poonville and the county attorney gets to work on him. Mary's father wants to get him a big city lawyer. George says any old lawyer will suit him. Some nice old guy with a beard. All the defense he needs is a map. The map is in George's head. Find the place where Joe was killed. Walk nineteen steps away from the river and turn sharp right and walk seven more and dig. "You'll find a busted gun buried in an oilskin shaving kit bag."

They find it. The gun is all blown to hell, except for the barrel, which is in fine shape, except that a piece of lead has been hammered down it with a punch.

The least the guy was asking for who fired that gun was a tin hand. But Joe was smart. He collected one hundred percent.

P.S. Something tells me George collected the girl, but I could be wrong.

A Case of Chivas Regal

GEORGE V. HIGGINS

*"Quotes make the story," George V. Higgins has
written, "so you damned right well better learn to
listen." He first showed his ability to listen—and
to write tough, convincing dialogue of the first
order—in* The Friends of Eddie Coyle *(1972).
Since then he has published ten novels (most recently* Penance for Jerry Kennedy, *1985), proving
his ability to write with verisimilitude about characters from the whole range of the legal system,
from the politicians who make the law to the
criminals who break it.*

*Asked to comment on "A Case of Chivas Regal,"
Higgins wrote: "The past decade or so has been a
worrisome time for the courts of justice. Media
have developed hypersensitivity to influence peddling, and the FBI, among other law enforcement
agencies, has made a cottage industry out of cap-
turing judges and court officers meddling with
cases. Judges are therefore very watchful that no
funny business occurs, and that vigilance, as Panda
says, leaves little room for human weakness—but
much for cleverness."*

*George Higgins began practicing law in 1967.
Now forty-five, he lives in Milton, Massachusetts.*

PANDA FEENEY, fifty-three, was employed as
a court officer. He escorted juries between
the courtrooms and the rooms where they deliberated,
and he made hotel and restaurant accommodations
for them when they were sequestered. He fetched
sandwiches and coffee for them when they were de-

liberating, and he delivered messages between them and the judges on their cases when they thought of silly questions during their deliberations. "But basically," Panda would say, "my job is to take care of the judges and do what they want, all right? What the judges want."

Panda did not like all of the judges that he served. Those he disliked made his back hurt, so he would disappear. He would stay somewhere around the second civil session, technically on duty but a little hard to find. It was not that he feared detection, loafing; he still remembered much of what he had learned wrestling, so he was indifferent to detection.

"My back," Panda would say, rubbing it, when some assistant clerk of courts located him bent over morning papers and a cup of coffee in the vacant jury room and said: "Judge wants to see you." Panda would nod painfully, writhing slowly in his chair. "Naturally, he wants to see me. Could've bet on it. Never fails: my back acts up, there's some guy like him in here. What's he want, huh? You know? Can you tell me that? This damp weather, Jesus, I can hardly move."

Clerks would never know what it was that judges wanted, only that they wanted Panda and had not seen him around. Panda would nod, once, when they told him that, and grimace. "Okay," he would say, "then can you do me a favor? Tell the judge: when I fought Casey—he has heard of Crusher Casey, even if he is a moron like he acts like he is—Crusher may've been an old guy, but he still had a body slam that ruined me for life. You can get the Judge's coffee for me, can't you? Do an old, lamed-up guy a favor? Tell him that for me."

One judge that Panda especially disliked was Henry Neelon. Before Judge Neelon was relieved of trying cases so that he could spend all of his time as the administrator of the courts, he had had a run-in with Panda Feeney. Panda after a few drinks would sometimes recall the story. "Hanging Hank'd spent the morning sending guys to Walpole. Handed out about a hundred years and still he wasn't satisfied. Gets back in his chambers and he's still looking to make trouble. Sends Grayson, that pinhead, out to look for me.

"I give Grayson the routine," Panda would say, chuckling. "Grayson'd believe anything you told him. He goes down and gives the word to Hanging Hank.

"Henry blows a gasket," Panda would say, laughing now. "He does not believe what Grayson tells him I said about my back, all right? He is going to check it out.

"I am sitting there, in the jury room. I can hear old Henry coming, stomping up those iron stairs and swearing like a bastard. He is going to take my head off. 'Lazy goddamned officers. Good-for-nothing shirkers.'

"So, I think quick," Panda said. "I don't have much choice. And when old Henry comes in, I am lying on the table. 'Damn you, Feeney,' he says, when he slams the door open, and then he sees me lying there like I am all set to be the guest of honor, my own wake.

Except I do not look as good as I will look when old Dave Finnerty finally gets me and lays me out in the front room. I've been holding my breath, so my face is red. And I have got a look on me like we used to use when the guy that's supposed to be the loser in the matches is pretending he is chewing on your leg, or pulling some other dirty trick that only bad guys do. Pain, you know what I mean? *Pain.* I am in agony— one look and you can see it. And Henry's jaw drops down.

'I dunno, Judge,' I say. I have got big tears in my eyes. 'I hate to even think about it, but the pain is awful. It doesn't stop, I'm gonna have to. Even though I don't want to, go on disability and just collect the pension. I may not have any choice.'

"Does he believe me?" Panda said. "At first, I guess he does. And then when he starts to suspect something, maybe I am jerking his chain, right? But he isn't sure. And even to this day, I catch him looking at me, he still thinks I was giving him the business that day I was on the table. And if he ever gets a shot at me again, that guy is gonna take it. I can see it in his eyes."

Panda Feeney liked Judge Boyster, so his back was always fine when Andrew Boyster drew his session. "Now you take someone like Drew Boyster," Panda would tell other judges when he served them the first time. "He is my idea, a judge. Not the kind of guy, you know, where everything is hard and fast and there's no allowances for human nature, you know? Drew Boyster is the kind of guy that I'd want judging me, if I was ever in that spot, which God forbid, I should be. If we had more like Andrew Boyster this would be a better world."

Andrew Boyster always squirmed when Panda's praise got back to him. "Ahh," he'd say, looking embarrassed, "I wish Panda wouldn't do that. Every new judge comes along, Panda gives indoctrination. And all it really means, I guess, is that I am too easy. I let Panda disappear, if I don't really need him—I suppose he's sleeping, but then, Panda needs his rest. Then too, I let Panda pick the hotels when the juries are sequestered, and the ones that Panda picks are always grateful for the business. He selects the restaurants when the juries sit through dinner, and he picks out the delis when they're having sandwiches. He's probably enriching pals, but then, should he pick those who hate him? And they probably show their appreciation in ways that might be worth some money. Nothing against the law, of course—I am not suggesting that. But I bet Panda has some trouble, paying for his dinners out." He did not tell Neelon that.

Panda's explanation differed. "You know why I like Drew Boyster?" He would squint when he said that, studying the novice judge for some sign of inattention. "He thinks I am smart, is why. He does not think I am stupid. Judge Boyster doesn't come in here, like lots of these guys do—and, Christ, you come down to it, some of the broads we get are worse. He doesn't just barge in here and start throwing weight around, acting like he owns the place and everybody in it. Drew Boyster

86

. . . well, I had one case he was involved in, before he became a judge. And that was all I needed, right? To see what kind of guy he is. This guy, he may be a lawyer and he made a lot of money before he went on the bench, although from what I heard, I guess his first wife made a big fat dent in that. But he has always had some class. Drew Boyster has got class. I have been here fifteen years. Judge Boyster is the best. I never ate a meal with him, or had a drink with him. It's not like we are buddies, you know? Or anything like that. It's just that, all the years I've been here, he's the best I ever saw."

He made that speech, with variations, to so many judges, that when Drew Boyster dropped dead at the age of fifty-nine, victim of a massive stroke that killed him instantly, Panda's name was mentioned by everyone who saw Judge Neelon on the morning afterward. Henry Neelon was in charge of making the arrangements for the speakers who would say a few words at Boyster's memorial, and as little as he liked the man, Henry Neelon saw the logic of including Panda Feeney.

"Look," he said, "I realize this may be hard for you. I know how you felt about Drew—everybody did."

Panda shook his head and looked down, as though he did not trust his voice to perform reliably.

"The thing of it is," Judge Neelon said to Panda, "you've been to enough of these things so you know what they are like. They are deadly, Panda—they are boring and they're dull. We get a couple lawyers who won recent cases in his court—we do not ask folks who lost. The Chief Justice declares on the record: 'He was not a pederast.' If he has one kid who can talk, we let the kid stand up—and then we all watch carefully to see if he breaks down, or displays any evidence that he's been using harmful drugs. For some reason, we don't ask surviving spouses to address us—it's probably because we're all afraid of what our own might say, if they got full attention, and we weren't there to reply. Then finally, one friend of his, if the dead guy had a friend, takes four or five long minutes to say nobody else knew him.

"You see what I mean, Panda?" Judge Neelon said pleadingly. "The last guy who gets up at those things is the only one who's right—none of the other speakers is a friend of the departed, someone who just *knew* him and enjoyed his company. No one that just *liked* him, unless he's another lawyer, ever gets a chance to speak. And we thought, since you did know Drew, and really did like him, maybe you would say a few words and do everyone a favor."

Panda looked up and he shook his head once more. "I couldn't do it, Your Honor," he said, and cracked his voice. "I would not know what to say. I'm not used to making speeches, standing up in public like that."

"Panda," Neelon said, "it could be very short. You could say . . . that case you had, the one that impressed you so much, you never forgot it? You could talk about that case, how Drew showed so much class. Look, you know Drew Boyster's history. You went back a ways with him. His family, they're not, you know, extremely happy with him, even now that he is dead. His kids, from everything I hear, they sided with the wife. You'd really help us out a lot if you saw your way clear to do it. Good Lord, Panda, all these years, you have drummed it into us. Just tell everybody once more, what a great guy Drew was."

"Your Honor," Panda said, coughing deeply as he started, "I have got to tell you—I can't talk about that case."

"Of course you can," Judge Neelon said. "It's on the public record. If it's the details that escape you, we can pull the files. We'll take care of that for you. That part will be easy."

"Judge," Panda said, "it wasn't that. It was not a case in court. Well, there *was* a case in court, that Judge Boyster was involved in. But the case I talked about . . . I can't talk about that."

"I don't follow you," the Judge said. He was starting to look grim.

"It was Chivas Regal," Panda said with difficulty. "A case of Chivas Regal, all right? That was what I meant."

"Scotch whiskey?" Neelon said. "A case of booze, you mean?"

Panda nodded. "Uh-huh," he said. "That was what it was."

"And this was back when Drew, when Drew was a lawyer?"

Panda nodded once again. "Yeah. Before he was a judge."

"Panda," Neelon said severely, "this is serious. Drew is dead now. It can't hurt him, not where he is now. But you're still escorting juries, and you still have access to them. If you influenced some verdict, back when Drew was practicing, and he gave you a case of scotch ... well, I don't have to tell you just how serious this is. What was it you did for Drew? Tamper with a jury, or do something dumb like that?"

Panda looked indignant. "Judge," he said, "I resent that. In all the years I've been here, I have never told a jury how they should vote in a case."

"Uh-huh," Neelon said, "well, you are the first one, then. But you've raised the suspicion now, and I am forced to deal with that. If you don't tell me the truth, and tell me the truth right now, I'll have to investigate and see what you did for Drew. And until I am satisfied, you will be suspended. Without pay, I might add, until this is all cleared up. Now which will it be, Panda? This is your decision now. You can tell me what went on, or you can leave this building right now and wait to hear from the D.A."

Panda looked more sorrowful than he had looked before. He had to clear his throat again. "This won't go any further?"

"It won't if there is nothing wrong," Judge Neelon said grimly. "If I think there is something wrong, it will go further, Panda. No promises apart from that. You understand me, Panda? And I will be the judge of whether you will be reported."

Panda sighed heavily. "All right," he said, "you got me. But there is nothing wrong with this, with what I did for Drew." Judge Neelon did not comment on that.

"Over twenny years ago, I got hurt in the ring."

"I know that," Neelon said. "Get on with you and Drew."

"I'm coming to that," Panda said. "Just give me a minute, will you? The doctors told me: 'Panda,' they said, 'this is it for grappling. You get hit like that again, you'll go out in a wheelchair. You are still a young man and your heart is pretty strong. You get crippled up for life, it is going to be a long one and you will have trouble working.'

"That scared the hell right out of me," Panda told Judge Neelon. "In wrestling there's no insurance. I did not have money. I was always undercard, a couple hundred bucks. And I didn't have any trade, you know. Something I could do. But I am scared, so what I do, I take what comes along. I get into security. I become a guard.

"The first job that I had," he said, "was in the Coast Apartments. This was before it was condo. This was 1963. And since I am new and all, I am put on nights. So I do not see who goes out—I just see who goes in.

"Now, Judge," he said, "I don't know just how I should put this to you. Because I don't want to shock you, or do anything like that. But lots of the big law firms then, had pads in those tall buildings. And on the tour they had me on, I'd see those guys come in. See them come in with their girlfriends? Between six and nine at night. And they would not go out again, 'fore I was through at one."

91

"Panda," Neelon said, "Spare me. You mean: 'With their nieces, they came in.' Learned counsel for rich law firms do not get so vulgar as to entertain mere girlfriends in deductible apartments."

"My mistake, Your Honor," Panda said. "Excuse me. On the tour they had me on, I often saw the lawyers come in with their nieces right behind them. Now, this took me a while, before I got this figured out. I was fairly innocent, when I stopped wrestling. And when I first started in there, I did not know much. So one night, this big honcho lawyer comes in with his briefcase, and it is six o'clock or so and I am pretty stupid. And also with him, right behind him, there is this young lady. A very fine looking young lady, I might add. And she has got her handbag, but that's all she's carrying. So I assume they're visiting someone— they do not live in the building, or else they would tell me. So I ask him: 'Which apartment?' Like I was supposed to do. Coast did not want people coming in there without they had destinations, and the people they were seeing wanted to see them.

'He gets all mad at me, the guy does," Panda said to Neelon. "He tells me he belongs to this firm which keeps an apartment there. Their clients in from out of town stay overnight in it. And sometimes in the evening, if they have a lot of work, they come in with their secretaries and they work late hours themselves. And that is what he's doing, and she is his secretary. 'Gleason, Boyster and Muldoon. That is all you need to know.' And they go on upstairs.

"Well, Your Honor, nothing happened. That I got in trouble for. This guy and his secretary, they go up to work late hours and I don't know who they are, except they work for a law firm that he says he belongs to. He don't say that he is Gleason and he don't claim he is Muldoon. I do not know he is Boyster and the lady had no name. All I knew her by was her looks, and like I told you, those were fine. She also had a nice smile and she always gave it to me.

"I say 'always,' Judge," he said, "and when I say that, I mean this: 'Wednesday nights she smiled at me.' Every Wednesday night. The first night was a Wednesday and then they come back, the next one. And I naturally remember them and I don't ask no questions. And then the Wednesday after that, and the one after that, until I see this is a habit, they got going here. This guy apparently can't get his work done, any Wednesday that you name. Tuesdays he's apparently all right, when they blow the quitting whistle. Thursdays he does not show up. I had Fridays off in those days, Fridays and Saturdays. He don't come in any Sunday. He does not show up on Monday. And by now I've gotten so I know a lot of guys that have problems just like his, except their big nights are different, and their secretaries change, or else they have got whole flocks of nieces like you would not have imagined. So I am wising up a little, and I'm keeping my mouth shut. And also I am putting my name in around the city, because I am getting older and those late hours are killing me.

"Anyway, two years go by, and then things start to change. I notice that this guy has started coming in on Tuesdays. And pretty soon it's Thursdays and I'm seeing him on Mondays, and when I come in on Sunday he's been working all weekend. His secretary, too— she's in there, and they're bringing in groceries. And then this other guy gets sick, so I have to cover for him, and damned if the secretary there and her boss are not working Friday nights and Saturday nights too."

"Thriving private practice," the Judge said, nodding at him. "Envy of every practitioner. Those hours are just brutal."

"They must be," Panda said. "Well, anyway, the days go by, and one day I am sitting there, I open up the paper. And what do I see but his picture and his name is under it. This is Attorney Andrew Boyster, who's been working those long hours. And he is in the paper because his wife's suing him. She is suing him in the back and she's suing his front, too. What she wants is a nice divorce, and every dime he's got. And there's another picture, which is of Andrew Boyster's wife. And she does not look like the lady that I know."

"She looked a little older, maybe?" Henry Neelon said.

"Well, I assumed she was," Panda Feeney said. "I didn't think too much about that, just how old she might've been. What caught my eye was, you know, she alleged adultery. And I thought I might have some idea, of just who she had in mind."

"Well," Feeney said, "the papers had their usual

field day. And I have got a dirty mind, so of course I read it all. And I am sitting there one night, the two of them come in, and I am looking at their pictures. They give me the great big grin, and she asks me how I like it.

"I do not know what to say. I figure they are going to tell me, I should mind my own damned business. So I mumble something at them, and they start to laugh at me. 'You're going to have to do better than that, if your name is Thomas Feeney,' Andrew Boyster says to me. And since we're never introduced, that kind of throws me, right? 'How come me?' I say to him, and that is when he tells me. I am getting a subpoena. I am going to testify.

"I say: 'Why me? What do I know?' He says his wife thinks that I know lots. Like who's been coming in and going out the building I am guarding, and she wants to ask me that.

"Now, I figure," Panda said, "I am in the glue for fair. So I ask him: 'What do I say?' And he says: 'Tell the truth.' And they go upstairs laughing, just as happy as can be. Which at least made me feel better, that the guy's not mad at me. I just may not lose my job."

"Did you testify?" the Judge said.

"Uh-huh," Panda said.

"And did you tell the truth?" the Judge said, looking grim again.

"Absolutely," Panda said. "Told the Gospel truth. Had on my best blue suit, you know, clean shirt and everything. And they ask me, his wife's lawyers, did I work the Coast Apartments and how long did I work there. I told him those things, truthfully, and all the other junk he asked me before he comes to the point. And when he does that he decides he will be dramatic. Swings around and points to Boyster and says: 'Do you know this man?' And I say: 'Yes, I do know him. That is Andrew Boyster.' Then he shows me a picture, which is Boyster's secretary that I guess is now his widow, and he wants to know: do I know her? And I say: 'Yes, I do.'

" 'Now,' he says, like this is this great big salute he's planned, 'how long have you known these people? Will you tell His Honor that?' And I say: 'Yessir. Yes, I will.' And I turn and face the Judge there and I say: 'I have known them for two weeks.' "

"Which of course was the strict truth," Neelon said, laughing with him. "Did he ask you the next question?"

"You mean: 'When did you first see them?' " Panda asked the Judge.

"Yeah," Judge Neelon said, "that is exactly what I mean."

"No," Panda said, "he didn't. I think he was flabbergasted. He just stood there and looked at me like his mouth wouldn't work. And then when he got it working, all he could think of asking me was whether I was very sure that was my honest answer. And I said: 'Absolutely, sir.' And then I was excused. And then when Christmas came that year, I got a case of Chivas Regal, and it was from Andrew Boyster and that second wife of his who I still think's a nice lady. And then when Drew got his judgeship, my name came up on the list faster than it ever would've otherwise, and that is how I got this job here. Because Drew thought I was smart. What I said, testifying, it did not make any difference to the way the case come out—at least that is what he told me. 'But,' he told me, 'Panda, it was the one laugh that we had while all that crap was going on, and we just wanted you to know that we appreciated it.' Which is why I thought Drew Boyster was a very classy guy—because of how he treated me."

Judge Neelon studied Panda for about a half a minute. Then he nodded and said: "Okay. You are off the hook. You don't have to speak when we have services for Drew. And I will not report you."

"Thank you, Judge," Panda said.

"There's one thing, though, I'd like to know," the Judge said thoughtfully. "At least, I think I'd like to know it, so I'll tell you what it is. That day when you were on the table, up there in the jury room? The day I burst in on you and you described your back pain to me in such colorful detail?"

"I remember it, Judge," Panda Feeney said.

"If I had asked you, that day, if you had that back pain then, what would you have told me? Do you want to tell me that?"

"To be candid, Judge," Panda Feeney said, "since you're giving me that option: No, I don't think that I do."

Neelon nodded. "Uh-huh," he said. "And if I were

97

to ask you: Have you ever lied to me? You'd tell me that you never have."

Panda Feeney nodded. "Yes. And that would be the truth."

Remember Mrs. Fitz!

GEORGE SIMS

George Sims lives in a village in Berkshire, England, where he is a dealer in modern rare books. The most recent of his eleven suspense novels, The Rare Book Game *(1985) draws on his thirty–year experience in the book trade.*

"I am incapable of writing a straightforward detective story because I am primarily interested in describing characters and conveying atmosphere," Sims comments. "Remember Mrs. Fitz!" substantiates this claim.

DEAR BARBARA BENYON,

I expect you have already peeked to see who this letter is from. Ha-ha! that was no good as you do not know me and I shall not put my given name but the one assigned to me from The Other Side. Yes, 'tis true, I am only an admirer from afar, but I do know quite a lot about you. For instance that you work at Barclays Bank, in the Strand branch—in fact it was to Messrs. Barclays that I was first indebted for your name, Miss Barbara J. Benyon, on that plaque which you so dexterously and prettily place on the counter.

But I am not one of your customers—I was only in the Strand branch on an errand or "a chore" as Mother used to say—so that will stop you puzzling as to which one I might be. What else do I know about you? Well, that you travel to and from the bank on the No. 11 bus and that you sometimes have lunch at Mario's on Agar Street. And occasionally you take sandwiches and eat them in Lincoln's Inn Fields or on the Embankment. Down by the Thames you tend to "moon about" and stare at the famous old river as if it might reveal some of its strange secrets to you, and I do think you are rather "the dreamy, romantic type." You have a tiny gold watch on a pigskin strap which you consult a good deal at lunch-time, and a gold locket, but no rings I'm glad to say! You are not tall, in fact "five foot two and eyes of blue." You recently had a summer cold. You read the Daily Mail on the bus in the morning and sometimes you buy the Standard on leaving the bank. All correct so far? Obviously I know where you live. By the way that girl who shares your flat is definitely not the type I should trust but more of that anon.

As for myself? Well I can't say too much at present but tallish and considered rather good-looking—if you like the dark, Romantic type. Perhaps more of a thinker than a man of action but reasonably outgoing with a good sense of humour, affectionate, responsive and above all sensitive! Much travelled and tanned!

I've been told that I'm inclined to be a bit suspicious, someone once said Paranoid (cheek!) and to search out other peoples' faults but I have not discovered any in you so far. May I be rather personal for a moment and say how much I like some of the frocks and suits you wear to work? But I can't say that I entirely approved of the rather revealing sunsuits you and your red-headed flat mate wore by the Serpentine last Sunday. And the horrid Lewd way she lay, exposing all she had got! She defintiely flaunts herself does that one and is obviously obsessed by the evil Serpent SEX. You see it is true, as Mother used to say, that some girls "have no sense of what is proper." They taunt men, lead them on and then are surprised when they end up in trouble! But that's the red-headed Tart's problem, not yours. I see that I've been led away by her disgusting goings-on from saying that in your grey dress, the navy one and the dark brown suit you remind me more than somewhat of my Mother and that is really the reason I have written to you. She had tiny feet like you. She always got her "Boots" as she called them at the fashionable Mayfair shop Pinet which was the only place where she could obtain the extra narrow size 3 fitting. I still have a pair of her "Boots" in a special case of which I'll tell you more some time. It is a very special case with three locks and a combination padlock so you can tell the contents must be important.

Well I must sign off now for "time's a-fleetin' "—

without of course any hope of a reply. Think of me just as a shadowy background figure, a humble patient sort of chap who does not intend to interfere with your life at all, but to remain watching over you with the very friendliest of intentions. Believe me ever

Sincerely yours
Laszlo

Dear Busy Bee,

Who sped away from Barclays Bank at lunch-time today and <u>not</u> on her usual stroll to Lincoln's Inn Fields or the Thames? Who verily raced along the Strand and past the Royal Courts of Justice (Justice! —that's a joke), then up Chancery Lane? Who had to jump out of the way of a mad lout in a careening black Bentley? Who went into Star Yard and entered the gloomy legal premises of Messrs. Castle, Harding & Walker? That's right—Barbara Busy Bee. And who followed her and waited ever so patiently outside? Yes—Faithful Laszlo. My Mother always told me that Patience was a great virtue. "Just wait and see." "Our turn will come," she used to say. I do hope that there was no very serious reason for you having to consult those legal codgers. If I had to hazard a guess, and it is something that I am rather good at, then I should say trouble at home. By which, of course, I mean trouble with that red-headed Tart <u>who takes men to your flat when you are not there!!</u> Not that I should dream of interfering there unless, of course, I sensed you wanted me to. Sometimes we all have to turn at bay!

I've been brooding on this troublesome, indeed worrying, problem of yours despite glares from an ugly, probably disease-ridden, Keeper in a Park which shall remain nameless. I must say that it is a shame you have been forced to go to Law to get that Tart out. "You can't trust the Law," Mother used to say. How right she proved to be! Patient, clever, resourceful, "a woman of most unusual qualities," as they admitted in Court, would you believe that such a woman could <u>end up dying in a prison cell?</u>

Yours sincerely
Laszlo

Dear Barbara Benyon,

Today, rather selfishly I suppose, I want to write about a matter which does tend to weigh me down a bit. I say selfishly because I know I should only be concerned with that Scarlet Woman flat mate who is making your life hell at the moment, and turning your flat into a noisome pit with her SEX goings-on. But this personal matter oppresses me somewhat and I just feel I must get some of it down on paper, set it straight for once and for all. Obviously you can't reply but I sense that you are "simpatico" and a trouble shared is a trouble halved. Anyway, see what you think.

A while ago now, I suppose it must be quite some years, against my father's wishes, I instigated a long series of seances for communication with the control Black Feather and Mother's mediumship.

The communicators who gave me the messages were the famous old Italian fiddle-maker Stradivarius and the Russian composer Rimsky-Korsakov. Up to that time you have my word for it that no messages from those illustrious gents had been received at our house! Strad who manifested first stated at once that he was sending the messages solely for me, and that I must collect them and write them all down, and that the financial results were to be solely for Mother and myself, and mainly for the purpose of assisting me and establishing me in my career. At hardly any of these seances was my father present!

Sorry if I have rambled on a bit but you know how it is, things do tend to get bottled-up over a period, particularly if you have no one to "chin-wag" with, and then it's best just to let off steam. Anyway, thanks again for listening.

Sincerely yours
Laszlo

Dear Barbara Benyon,

Today I was very touched to see you looking pale and cast down with care—all because of the terrible troubles that the red-headed whore has brought upon you. She is definitely SEX mad—I know the type!

Of course I noticed that you did not go out with her this Sunday even though the sun was baking hot. Very wise. Take my tip and keep away from her as much as possible until the creaking, slow-grinding Law at last compels her to leave your flat! I noted by the way that she has now got some oily looking chap, probably her Pimp, to accompany her to and from work. But her time will come so please do try and cheer up. Forget her and that will undoubtedly bring the roses back into your cheeks.

Sincerely yours
Laszlo

Dear Barbara Benyon,
Only me! Yes, verily, I am doubly blessed. Fortunate indeed to have the famous Black Feather as my control—yes, you're right, the very same Black Feather who was once "left-hand control" for the illustrious Madame Eusapia Palladino. And dear old Strad who manifests so readily, really "at the drop of a hat." Rimsky is much more difficult I'm afraid, and sometimes seems to be sulking, but I suppose he is still much tied up with music matters on The Other Side.

Barbara—we are both, there's no point in being falsely modest, generously endowed with blessings. However I do sometimes wonder if you may not be the type who accepts same without much thought for others less fortunate.

A friend of mine is a case in point. He happens to

be smallish. For that reason he had to take humble employment—definitely not in keeping with his education, upbringing, family background, etc. This friend of mine was always most methodical, patient and anxious to please. But the men in the place where he worked were immediately jealous of him and could see that the Boss took a friendly interest in him and that he was well placed for early promotion. So they started a campaign! Threats, hints, lies and abuse! They tried a number of plots which all failed miserably. Vile libels, etc! The last straw was the planting of stolen goods! A fiendish set-up you say? But would you credit that such a chap would get his own back on that foul gang of toughs? Well he did! With Strad's help! They certainly reaped the whirlwind, or should I say the furnace? Ha-ha! I'll tell you all about it one day.

I don't think I ever finished off the tale about the Rev. Gent my father. Through a foul trick he published all those confidential chats with Strad and Rimsky on his own!! <u>This meant the loss of ten years' work!</u> After a lot of wrangling father gave us a signed contract that we should receive 50% of the profits. And a signed confession of his own free will. Strad said that compromise was the only way and I thought we should listen to the wise old fiddle-maker. So, all serene. Then—what do you think? Father decamped, a moonlit flit no less, with that precious contract and confession. Now you may have some inkling of what Mother went through at that precious Vicarage! We of course wrote to the publishers insisting that a clause should be put in the contract to allow us a percentage. Result?—no reply.

What a nice new black dress! And I was glad to see the way you ignored that crude oaf who wanted to maul you in getting off the bus this morning. Don't think that we are all like that (SEX mad).

Yours sincerely
Laszlo

Dear Barbara Benyon,

May a comparative stranger give you a word of advice? Fairly blunt but with the very best of intentions withal. Don't encourage strange men by smiling at them. Now you see how closely I have you under observation.

Yours sincerely
Laszlo

Dear Barbara Benyon,

Did I ever tell you about Mrs. Fitz? Not her real name of course, I'm rather careful about such things. She definitely "took a shine" to me. Of course I could see some of her faults, at least some of the physical ones, from the start. Those great thick legs with ankles that bulged over her size 9 plates of meat—it amused her to contrast them with my own very neat size fives.

That none-too-clean neck and oh those hairy moles! But something about her manner, at first she feigned a quiet modesty, reminded me of Mother. Later on I found out her true nature—how greedy she was—and other things!

Mrs. Fitz lived all alone like a hermit in a great big dark house, but pigged it in only two rooms, never cleaning anything and hardly ever washing her crocks. It was a very gloomy house with big trees that shut out the light and the garden was all overgrown with weeds. Every single room in the house was full of junk. She never threw anything away and there were hundreds of empty bottles and piles of tins and bags in the kitchen. Another pile of unread newspapers and un-opened letters in the hall. There was so much stuff in some rooms that you couldn't get into them. I only hung around there as she promised to set me up in my career.

In a hurry so I must close.

By the way am I mistaken or is someone following you? <u>I mean someone apart from me of course.</u>

Sincerely yours
Laszlo

Dear Barbara Benyon,
"Suffocated with a pillow!" I hear you exclaim your doubt and derision at the very suggestion. Yes, indeed,

how could they be sure? Who is to say that the Rev.
Gent did not suffocate himself? One thing is certain—
Mother was quite innocent! But you see Strad says
there is no justice in this world. He says that on The
Other Side all is different. Sometimes, I must admit, I
do rather long to be there.

Ever sincerely
Laszlo

Dear Miss Benyon,

Just to say that I am definitely on to the blonde beast
who is now your constant companion and his Jewboy
friend. Are the police really recruiting Yids now? Well
they must be hard up if they stoop to having Kikes
working for them! The police would be well advised to
keep out of my affairs. Where do they all skulk when
they are really needed?

One tries hard only to think of pleasanter subjects
but under pressure it is difficult. Oh yes I was telling
you about Mrs. Fitz (not her real name so no investi-
gations about that by request please). Would you
believe she had kept all her old toys and those of her
long-dead brother? On the sideboard in the dining-
room there were long lines of toy soldiers smothered
in dust. One afternoon she fell asleep, looking a disgusting sight with her large mouth wide open and
showing her denture plate. I explored the whole place
and decided on a plan.

Feeling rather down and "put upon." However Strad says "Not to worry."

Faithfully yours
Laszlo

Dear Miss Benyon,

Today when you stopped to buy your Standard you were carrying a small parcel. Blonde beast was wearing a shoddy blue suit while Jewboy skulked along behind, looking furtive and ashamed of himself. Now you can see you are all closely observed.

At no time did dear old Strad speak to my father!

Shall I give you a clue as to my present whereabouts? A café in the Strand not a million miles from Barclays Bank & Barbara Benyon. I can say that as I shall not come here again. A giant of a pimply waitress flicked some crumbs on me.

Strad has just come through loud and clear. Danger ahead! So I'm off. Your bullies are even worrying Strad now but I don't suppose that bothers you.

Faithfully yours
Laszlo

Dear Miss Benyon,

We wrote to the publishers on countless occasions in re the Rev. Gent and his claims that Strad had first manifested to him.

Had to move in a rush as you undoubtedly gleefully heard and lost all my notes regarding the trial. Also various files of useful information, OFFICIAL DOCUMENTS and other valuable possessions. A savage blow but I keep trying to look on the bright side.

Did I ever tell you about that terrible woman Mrs. Fitz? That's what I called her as she thought she was "out of the top drawer" all right. Lording it like Lady Muck. Behaved as if she was made of money but had hardly anything apart from that old house which she could not sell as it was riddled with dry rot. She didn't wash but smothered herself in cheap scent. And the house stank because all the windows were closed and nailed up fast. She was scared stiff of burglars!

Father said that he would have to take legal proceedings. That he was determined to stop us "making his life a misery." We soon settled his hash!

Faithfully
Laszlo

Miss Benyon,

Not to mince matters your louts are making <u>my</u> life a misery! In a second rush move I lost Mother's precious case! I am definitely being hounded. Not a nice feeling. I have written to the Papers and the Authorities about this sort of thing before but nothing is ever published as they are all in cahoots.

<u>I stake my reputation on the authenticity of Strad's</u>

<u>messages.</u> But for say £100 I would have been willing to relinquish all rights. This letter is a jumble because of your loathsome bullies.

> Faithfully
> Laszlo

Benyon,
    Mrs. Fitz was disgusting. I stuck it out there even when she tried to make a fool of me by sitting me on her lap—just like a ventriloquist's dummy. She said she was sincerely interested in The Other Side and promised to help me with my career. She even wanted to act as my medium—as if I would ever use anyone apart from Mother! Finally I realised that all she was interested in was SEX. So I tied her up when she was sleeping and forced her head down the lavatory pan to stop her snoring. Then I smashed everything in the house and emptied every tin and jar in the kitchen. Then I left all the taps running. That showed her, eh!
    Of course the police lied when they said Mrs. Fitz was dead. They were just trying to frighten me, to hound me like they did my sainted Mother, "a woman of most unusual qualities" as that Fiend/Judge was forced to admit.
    Strad <u>insists</u> that I "go underground" for a while. All this anxiety on top of losing the case containing

Mother's "Boots" is just too much to bear. I sincerely advise you to call off your hounds. Anyway they are sure to lose interest if I lie doggo for a while. Then I shall return. Remember Mrs. Fitz!

> Ever faithfully
> Laszlo

Trouble in Paradise

ARTHUR LYONS

Jacob Asch was introduced in Arthur Lyons's first novel, The Dead Are Discreet (1974), *and in the eight Asch novels since, Lyons has written so convincingly about crime that he has been engaged as a consultant by the Los Angeles Police Department.*

"Trouble in Paradise," Lyons reports, "was inspired by a true case I learned of while doing research for a book in the Caribbean. Being a scuba diver myself, I was fascinated by the case, and although my version of what happened differs from the outcome of the actual case, I feel that this is the way it could have come down. It is the only Jacob Asch story in print."

Arthur Lyons lives in Palm Springs, California, where he operates a restaurant called Lyons' English Grill. He is thirty-nine.

"THAT WHORE DID IT," John Anixter proclaimed angrily. "I know she did. I want you to prove it."

He was a tall and gristly forty-odd, with a long, rectangular face and brown hair that was deciding to be gray. His eyes were pale blue and had a no-nonsense expression in them. His dress was no-nonsense, too; a gray worsted suit, a white shirt, and a gray and blue striped tie. His hands were jewelryless except for an inexpensive Seiko watch. All in all, he looked no more than a fairly prosperous businessman; I would have had no idea he was worth $8 million if Harry Scranton hadn't told me.

Harry was an attorney for whose firm I occasionally did investigative work and the one who had recommended me to Anixter. All that he had told me about the man, except for how much money he had, was that he had made it dabbling in the commodities market before starting up his own successful commodities brokerage firm, and that he was a hell of a nice guy. Oh yeah, he also told me that the man's son had recently died in an accident, which was why he wanted to see me.

"What whore is that, Mr. Anixter?"

His face flushed. "The one Chip married. He couldn't see what she was, but it was obvious to me the first time I laid eyes on her."

"Chip was your son?"

He nodded, then turned and looked out the window. The office was plush, with elm burl walls adorned by deco light sconces and furnished with big, cushy chairs with great wide arms. "When I cut Chip off," Anixter said, looking down the fourteen floors to the streets of Century City, "I thought for sure she would take the hint and leave, but she found another way to work it."

He was trucking now and I was peddling slowly behind on my bicycle. I peddled harder, trying to catch up. "Work what?"

He turned and gave me a solemn look. "Three

months ago, my son took out a life insurance policy worth $300,000, with her as the beneficiary. Two months later, Chip died under mysterious circumstances while scuba diving in the Caribbean. The authorities in St. Maarten have declared it an accident, but I'm certain that woman had something to do with it. Chip was an experienced diver and a super athlete. Scuba was one of his passions. She probably worked some sort of deal with the scuba instructor to do away with Chip and split the money."

"Was an autopsy performed?"

"You have to have a body to perform an autopsy."

"They never found his body?"

He shook his head. "All they found was his diving gear and swim trunks. Both were pretty chewed up."

"Sharks?"

He shrugged.

One thing I have found with parents whose children have died unnaturally, murder is always a preferable alternative to suicide or accidental death. With the former comes a truckload of guilt and with the latter comes a capricious and uncaring universe.

"The insurance company has to have investigators on it, Mr. Anixter—"

He waved a hand in exasperation and sat back down at the desk. "There's nothing they can do. Chip's death is officially an accident. In the absence of new evidence, they're going to have to pay off." Two knots of muscle rose on his jawline, just below his ears. "I'll see that bitch in hell before I let her collect a bounty on my son's life."

"How long were they married?"

"Five months." He leaned back in his chair, and his brow furrowed. "My son was a screw-up, Mr. Asch."

"The only thing he ever showed any interest in was fast cars and faster women. A lot if it was my fault, probably. I wasn't the best father in the world. My wife—Chip's mother—died when he was only nine and I was too busy trying to keep the business going to give him the supervision he needed. When he was a teenager, I had to get him out of one scrape after another. I always thought he would straighten up, even after he quit college and drifted from one job to another. I offered him a position with my company, but he said he had to 'find himself,' whatever that means. But when he came to me and said he intended to marry that tramp, that was the last straw."

He paused, but he wasn't through yet. He came forward and rested his forearm on the desk.

"I've worked my butt off my whole life, Mr. Asch. I came up from nothing and struggled to put something together. Too damned hard to sit back and watch it squandered on some fortune-hunting hooker. I told Chip if he wanted to marry the girl, fine, but he could support her on his own, because he wouldn't get one more dime from me, before or after I died. We both said things we shouldn't have. That was the last time I saw him." Coldness in the blue eyes softened; guilt tugged at his features.

"You called the woman a hooker," I said. "Did you mean that literally?" He gave a look of distaste. "They all hook in places like that."

"Places like what?"

"The Paradise," he said, folding his hands on the desk top. "It's a topless bar on Beverly Boulevard. She was dancing there when Chip met her."

I wrote it down. "What's her first name?"

"Rhonda," he said, as if he did not like the sound of the word.

"Where is she living now?"

"In Chip's apartment." He recited the address, then looked at me appraisingly as if I were a pork belly for which he was trying to guess tomorrow's market value. "Harry says you're good."

Never one to deal well with flattery, I said nothing.

"That bitch took away my only son," he said through pursed lips. "I don't care how much money it takes, I want her nailed for it."

It sounded as if he had lost his son years ago and wanted me to help him pin his guilt on the woman. For two hundred a day plus expenses, I was willing to at least try.

"I'll see what I can do," I said.

Chip and Rhonda Anixter had gotten married in September, in Westwood, and I obtained a copy of the marriage license from the Hall of Records downtown. Her maiden name was Rhonda Jo Banks, and she was twenty-eight, two years older than Chip. She had been born in Arizona, had completed high school, and listed her occupation as "dancer." I figured that was as good a place to start as any.

The Paradise was on Beverly Boulevard, on the edge of the Silver Lake district, in the middle of a fatigued city block of laundromats and seedy-looking Mexican and Vietnamese restaurants. From the outside, it looked like a dirty plywood and plaster box, covered with cartoon paintings of leggy, scantily-clad girls. Inside, it was a dirty plywood and plaster box with real girls instead of cartoons. The cartoons looked better.

The place was built like a dog pit, with tables set around the perimeters of the sunken dance floor, where an anemic-looking redhead in nothing but a G-string was gyrating listlessly to a Michael Jackson tune. "Flashdance" it wasn't.

Afternoon trade was sparse and I had no trouble securing a table. Passing myself off as an old acquaintance of Rhonda's, it took one hour, five beers and twenty-eight dollars in "tips" spread between the bartender and a bovine brunette named Noreen to find out Rhonda had not been around much since she'd gotten married. Noreen was particularly talkative, especially after I picked up some latent hostility from her and assumed the role of one of Rhonda's jilted ex-boyfriends.

"Don't feel like the Lone Ranger," she said in a snide tone, the hostility becoming less latent as she talked. "You're in some good company. She was going out with the owner of the club, Arnie Phalen, when she met that rich kid. The minute she found the kid had bucks, she dumped Arnie on his ass. Strutted around here bragging how she was going to set herself up for life with that score. I guess the joke was on her."

"Why is that?"

The corners of her mouth turned up in a self-satisfied leer. "She came back in a few months ago, crying to Arnie about how the kid was broke. The kid's old man was the one with the money and he'd cut them off on account of her I guess. He had about as much use for her as a case of herpes."

"She been back in since then?" I asked, sipping my beer.

"Naw," she said, waving a hand disparagingly. "She's too good for this place. All she did when she worked here was bitch her whole shift about what a dive this place was and how she was gonna make a score and get out. She must have thought she was Grace Fucking Kelly or something, the way she acted."

"Arnie around now?" I asked casually.

She shook her dark, ratted hair. "He doesn't come in till around seven." She looked down at the blond dancing in the pit and said, "I'm up." I took out my wallet. "Thanks for the conversation, Noreen," I said, and left her an extra five as a tip, just for public relations in case I needed to talk to her again.

Her changebox snapped up the bill and she smiled warmly. She had a live one now. "My shift is over at six," she said. "Stop back then and maybe we can have a drink or something."

"Maybe I'll do that."

When I left, she was moving her big body to Bob Seger's "Fire Down Below," and she threw me a few hip-pumps and breast-flops as I went out the door.

The Anixter's ex-connubial love nest was in a new, two-story, vanilla-colored apartment building on a tree-lined street of apartments scissored out of the same nondescript mold. After making sure that the red Porsche Carrera John Anixter had bought his son for his twenty-first birthday was in its slot in the garage, I went back around front, and through the glass doors. At the edge of the swimming-pool courtyard, I stopped.

A lone woman was sunning herself in one of the deck chairs by the pool, and I knew instinctively it was Rhonda. She had on a tiny string bikini, and her tanned body glistened with oil. She had a hard, flat stomach and long, slim legs, and maybe a little too much in the chest department, but being the magnanimous person that I was, I figured I could live with that. Her face, although not as spectacular as her body, was a solid 8, framed by a mane of ash blond hair. She shifted languorously onto her stomach and I wiped a hand across my chin and checked for drool. I could see why Chip had ignored his father's advice.

Figuring that if she intended to go out anywhere it wouldn't be for a while, I went back to the car and drove to Carl's Jr., where I grabbed a quick infusion of cholesterol with cheese, and was back in place across the street within half an hour. I found a jazz station and settled back with my styrofoam cup of coffee. Shadows lengthened, cars went by, cars pulled in and out of the driveway to the apartment building, but she was not in any of them. It was almost dark when a black Corvette cruised by slowly, and parked in a space a few cars up.

There was something about the man who got out of

the Vette that attracted my attention. Maybe part of it was the shades he was still wearing, despite the thickening dusk; the sun is always shining when you're cool. He was short and weaselly-looking, with a thin, olive–complected face and . oily black hair slicked straight back from his high forehead. To go with the shades, he wore a gray sports jacket over a black shirt, jeans and white tennis shoes. He didn't notice me watching him across the street; he was a man on a mission.

I waited until he was through the glass doors of the building before I got out of the car and followed. By the time I got to the mailboxes, he was on the other side of the pool, disappearing through a door into the building. The door opened into a corridor and he was standing in front of a door halfway down it. He glanced at me as I went past him, pretending to be looking at apartment numbers, and then Rhonda Anixter's door opened and he went inside.

I hurried back outside. The Corvette was locked, so I contented myself with taking down the plate number, and went back to my car. At two-fifteen, I was rudely awakened by the sound of an engine starting. I slouched down while the Corvette flipped a U and roared up the block toward Overland. I pulled out with my lights off and drove that way until we picked up some traffic. He got on the freeway at Overland and headed north to the Wilshire exit, where he got off. At Barrington he made a right and half a dozen blocks up, turned into the driveway of a single-roofed, ranch-style house with a lot of trees in the front yard.

He had taken off his shades and was locking up the Corvette when I drove past. The house was dark and there was a yellow compact of some sort parked in front of the Vette. Up the block, I stopped and jotted down the address, counted to one thousand, then went back on foot.

At the neighbor's hedge, I crouched down and peeked into the front yard of the house. There was no sign of Mr. Cool, and I assumed from the faint glow behind the curtains of the living room window that he had gone inside. I stood up and sauntered by as if it were perfectly normal to be out for a casual stroll at three in the morning, then went into a crouch on the other side of the driveway and used the body of the Corvette as a cover to reach the yellow car.

It was a Nissan. I took down the plate number, then duck-walked to the door on the passenger side. It was locked, of course. My flash located the registration attached to the sun visor in a leather-framed case. I leaned close to the window to get a look.

Barbara Phalen
777 Barrington
Brentwood, CA.

Barbara Phalen. Arnie Phalen's wife? Maybe Phalen was making a comeback, now that Chip was out of the picture. Maybe he had never left.

I snapped off the flash and something hard and small and cold pressed against the back of my head. The hammer clicking back sounded like a sonic boom.

"Just straighten up nice and easy, asshole," a voice said quietly.

I did as I was told. I didn't know what caliber the gun was, but at that range, a pellet gun would have muddled some of my fondest memories.

"If you're thinking of getting cute," the voice said, "you'll never think again." A hand slammed me into the car and the gun moved down to poke me in the kidney.

"Easy." I said, the pain straightening me up.

"Fuck you. Stand back and spread your feet and put your hands on the top of the car."

I did it and his free hand patted me down. It brushed my wallet and plucked it from my inside pocket. The pressure of the gun went away as he stepped back to inspect it. "Turn around," he said after a moment.

Without the shades he lost some of his weaselly look. He was not bad looking, in fact, in a greasy kind of way. His eyes were dark and deeply set. In the dim light from the house, they were devoid of any emotion except for a mildly contemptuous curiosity. "All right, peeper, what the hell are you doing sneaking around here?" The corner of his mouth twitched.

"I'm on a case."

"What case?"

I considered that for a moment. "A little girl hired me to track down her lost Lhasa Apso. Named 'Button,' as in 'cute as a?' Maybe you've seen him. About a foot tall, blond hair, brown eyes—"

The twitch stopped and tightened into an angry line. He pointed the gun at my head again. "You know who you're fucking with, asshole? I could have you made into an ashtray if I wanted to. Now, I'm gonna ask you again: What case?"

I pointed at the gun. "Why don't you put that thing down? I have trouble talking when I'm nervous." I was sweating; he seemed to like that.

One side of his mouth lifted into a lopsided, self-confident sneer. "You'll find a way."

I had nothing to lose, so I threw out a guess. "Your wife hired me to find out where you go when you're supposed to be watching tits bounce up and down. I wonder what she's going to say when I tell her you're watching them okay, but the wrong set?"

The confidence on his face dried up and flaked off like a month-old Christmas tree. "You're a liar."

It was my turn to smile. "Let's get her out here and ask her."

He shot a troubled look at the house, then back at me.

"Of course, I'm always open for a better offer."

"What kind of an offer?" he asked in a clipped voice.

"That's open for discussion."

The porch light above the front door went on and his head snapped around. A woman's voice called out from the crack in the door: "Arnie?"

I looked at Phalen's panicked face. He was the one who was sweating now. "Well?"

"Get out of here," he whispered, his voice thick with hate.

I held out my hand. "My wallet."

He hesitated, and Barbara Phalen called out again: "Arnie?"

"Coming, hon," he called back, and tossed the wallet at me. In a hoarse whisper, he said: "Move your ass out of here. Quick."

"I'll be in touch," I told him, and hurried down the driveway. At the sidewalk, I turned left and used the other side of the street to circle back to my car so she wouldn't see me.

All the way home, I chewed myself out for my carelessness. But it was more than just the fact that Phalen and Rhonda now knew they were being watched that bothered me; it was Phalen himself. The man was bad news, I could feel it. Maybe it was the comfortable way he handled a .38 or the dead eyes and the hard sneer, or the silent, deadly way he'd pounced on me. And now he knew who I was. I figured I'd better find out who he was before he made good on his threat and I wound up a receptacle for some Mustache Pete's cigar.

I got up at nine, not wanting to. I'd spent a fitful night being pursued by various people and things, and although I didn't remember exactly who they were or why they were pursuing me, there had been a lot of running and jumping done, and I woke up exhausted. Figuring that if I was going to be chased around in my sleep I should probably know by whom, I went into the kitchen and made a pot of coffee and drank half of it before calling Sheriff's Homicide.

Al Herrera sounded chipper when he picked up the phone. I was glad to hear that; the last few times we'd talked he had sounded as if he were ripe for a stress disability.

Al and I went way back to my reporting days at the *Chronicle*, and if I had changed a lot since then, he hadn't. He was still the same thick-skinned, straight-shooting, 100 percent cop, which was probably to his detriment. He took the job too seriously and had nearly suffered a couple of emotional and marital breakdowns because of it. "Jake boy, where you been keeping yourself?"

"On my knees, Al, looking through keyholes. How are things with you?"

"Great, if you like being up to your ass in dead bodies."

After the obligatory small talk—how's the wife and kids, that sort of thing—I sprung it. "Al, I need a favor—"

"Of course. Why else would you call?"

I told him that for a Mexican, he did a passable imitation of a Jewish mother, then gave him all the information I had on Phalen and Rhonda Anixter and asked him to run them for priors.

"And you need it done yesterday, right?"

"Today would be all right."

He said he would be in the field until four or so and

to call back then and I hung up and thought about my next step. Deciding a little soft-shoe might be appropriate, I dropped another quarter and dialed Rhonda Anixter's number. Her voice was as sultry as her body —husky and vaporous.

"Mrs. Rhonda Anixter?"

"Yes?"

"This is Bob Exley at the Collection Department of Pacific Bell. I'm calling to inform you, Mrs. Anixter, that unless we receive immediate payment for last month's bill, your phone will be disconnected on the first—"

The huskiness turned into a growl. "What the hell are you talking about? I paid that bill two weeks ago."

"What was the date and number of the check and at what bank do you have your checking account?"

"Security National, West L.A. Pico branch," she said in a vexed voice. "I'll have to look up the number."

"Just a minute, Mrs. Anixter, that may not be necessary. Running this through again, I see that the computer posted your check late, for some reason. I'm very sorry to have bothered you."

"Sure you are," she said in a nasty tone, and hung up.

I called Troy Wilcox. Troy was chief loan officer at L.A. First Federal, and two years ago, while working on an entirely different matter, I'd saved his ass when I tumbled onto a man who had skipped on a $75,000 bank loan Troy had okayed for him. Ever since, Troy had always been pleased to help me out with a favor when I needed one. And just as he would be pleased to do me a favor, the people at Security National would be pleased to do him one. There is no such thing as privileged information in the banking fraternity.

I was batting a thousand today; Troy was in a good mood, too. I gave him Rhonda Anixter's name and told him him I needed to know if she had written any checks for sizeable amounts in the past two months, and if so, to whom. He told me to get back to him a little before three, that he should have the information by then.

Since there didn't seem to be anything else to do until that time, I went home to pack.

Both Al and Troy were ready for me when I got back to them that afternoon, and on the red-eye to Miami, I mulled over what they had given me.

Chip and Rhonda's joint account at Security National showed a balance of $746.98. Only two checks of any sizeable amount had been written by either of them in the past two months, one on September 1 to Wynee World Travel for $3500, which would have been for the Caribbean trip, and another a week later to "Cash," for $2000, which was more than likely for vacation spending money. I hadn't really expected Troy to come up with anything incriminating; if Rhonda Anixter had paid someone to kill her husband and make it look like an accident, she wouldn't have been likely to write him a check from their joint account.

Al's stuff was more interesting. Rhonda had no record in California, but the Vice boys knew all about

Phalen. Besides being the owner on record of the Paradise, Phalen was part-owner and front man for two other topless bars that were suspected of being laundries for mob money; he was also the main man at New Eros, a distributor of hard-core porn films and magazines. He had been popped three times—for extortion, pandering, and burning with intent to defraud an insurer—but never convicted. That last one particularly interested me. The arrest report had been filed by the Sheriff's Office, and I asked Al if he could pull it for me. After three-and-a-half minutes of bitching and moaning about how busy he was, he finally agreed, but said it would take a couple of days. I told him I'd be in touch, threw my bag in the car, and drove out to LAX.

My flight didn't leave until eleven-ten, and the three double-vodkas I absorbed in the airport terminal bar and the two more I ingested on the plane allowed me to sleep straight through to Miami. After a two-hour layover there and another three hours on an Eastern 727, I was sober, awake, and buckling up for a landing in St. Maarten.

From the air, one side of the island didn't look any different from the other—it just looked like one tiny green teardrop surrounded by a blue-green sea that seemed to change color on a whim—but according to the Caribbean guidebook I'd picked up in the Miami airport gift shop, St. Maarten/St. Martin had the distinction of being the smallest island in the world with two sovereignties. The French and Dutch both settled the island in the early 1600s, and legend had it that instead of fighting for possession, they'd decided to divvy it up by a walking contest. One man from each side walked around the island in opposite directions, and where they met determined the border. I hoped the resolution of my current case would be as peaceful.

I checked in at the Sheraton near the airport and caught a cab into Philipsburg, the Dutch capital. It was a cloudless, balmy day in the small, dusty town strung out along a sandbar that ran between the sea and a large salt marsh. Front Street, the main drag, was narrow and congested with cars and people, and the cab seemed to make about four feet an hour.

I tried to get into the laid-back Caribbean mentality by sightseeing out the window.

The town had an eclectic ambiance to it, which was a nice way of saying it was a mish-mash of architectural styles. Modern glass-sheeted shopping malls were stuck between old, pastel painted, colonial-style buildings and slat wood, front-porched houses. No matter how different the buildings were in appearance, they all had the same function—to sell to the shorts-clad, window-gaping army of tourists laden with cameras and chicly imprinted shopping bags as they thronged the sun-drenched sidewalks.

The police station was one of the older colonial buildings, at the end of Front Street. After identifying myself to the desk sergeant, I was turned over to a surly black cop named Cribbs who had handled the Anixter investigation. His attitude thawed a bit when I assured him I had not come all this way to question his competence, rather to consult his expertise.

Chip Anixter's diving equipment was in a storage room in back. There was a weight belt, an air tank with the regulator still attached, and what was left of a pair of trunks. The trunks were shredded but the eight or nine cuts in the weight belt looked too clean to have been made by any fish. When I mentioned that to Cribbs, he just shrugged, and said in his West Indian accent, "You ever see a shark's teeth? They are as sharp as razor blades." There didn't seem to be any point in arguing with him. Besides the lacerations in the weight belt and the fact that the tank was empty of air when it was found, the equipment checked out okay and did not seem to have been tampered with in any way.

The diving instructor Chip had gone down with, Stuart Murphy, was a California transplant who had come to St. Maarten eight years ago and started Mako Water Sports, an operation specializing in recreational dives. Except for Chip, the company had a perfect safety record, and Cribbs considered Murphy beyond suspicion. As for Rhonda Anixter, Cribbs thought her "cold" considering what had happened, but that was no crime. She couldn't have had anything to do with the accident, because she had never left the boat during the dive. The entire incident was an unfortunate accident, but that was all it was. I thanked him and left.

Mako Water Sports was in a small wooden building that sat at the edge of a yacht marina. The desk inside was surrounded by racks of life vests, regulators, and air tanks. The man sitting behind it was a rangy, freckled, beachy type with a bleached-out mustache and pink splotches on his prematurely balding head where the skin had sunburned and peeled off. He wore swim trunks and a short-sleeved shirt covered with red hibiscus.

"I'm looking for Stu Murphy."

"You've found him," he said, smiling broadly. He had a lot of nice, white teeth.

"My name is Asch." I handed him a card. "I'm down here working on the Anixter case. I'd like to ask you a few questions, if you could spare a little time—"

He looked at the card and frowned. "I'm afraid I can't. I'm very busy."

I looked around the room. There didn't seem to be too much happening in it.

"I told everything I know to the police," he said, picking up my skeptical look. "Why don't you talk to them?"

"I did. They absolved you of all guilt in the matter. That's not why I'm here. There is a lot of insurance money involved and Chip's father is concerned that his son's death might have been the result of foul play. Was there anything that struck you as peculiar about his disappearance?"

"Yeah," he said sourly. "The whole damned thing. Believe it or not, mister, I'm not used to having my clients disappear on me."

"That wasn't what I was implying."

He made a face and let out a breath. "Look, I don't mean to sound rude. But all I want is to put this thing behind me." He waved a hand at the room. "It wasn't exactly the greatest publicity for my business, as you can see."

I took out my wallet, extracted a fifty-dollar bill, and laid it on the desk in front of him. "Would that cover a quick run out to where Chip disappeared? No equipment. We wouldn't even have to break the surface."

"What do you expect to see from the surface?"

"I don't know," I said, truthfully.

He looked at the money, bit his lip thoughtfully, then put his hand over the bill and slid it toward him. He stood and went over to the rack of life vests, selected one, and tossed it at me. "You'd better put this on. If I lose one more client, I might as well close this place up and go back to the States."

The trade winds were kicking up a good chop and my clothes were soaked by the time Murphy killed the engine of the speedboat and dropped anchor. "This is it," he said.

We were two or three miles offshore and the water was dark blue, not green as it was in the sandy shallows closer to the island. The sunlight was clean and hard and glinted white off the surface of the sea. I looked down.

"How can you tell this is the exact spot?"

He smiled cryptically. "It's my business."

I let it go at that. "You two went down alone?"

He nodded. "He didn't want to out with a group. Wanted a more personal dive, he said."

"What kind of a diver was he? Good?"

The welcome warmth of the sun seeped through my wet clothes, taking the chill off.

"So he said. He was certified."

"So what happened?"

"Good question. One minute, he was behind me, the next, he wasn't. The only thing I can think of is that he got absorbed in something and got carried away by the current without realizing. It's pretty strong here."

"If the current is so strong, why did you pick this spot to dive?"

"I didn't," he said. "He did."

"When was that?"

"The day before, when he came into the office. He said a friend of his wife who dove around here all the time recommended it."

A mill wheel in my mind turned a notch and caught. "A friend of his wife?"

"That's what he said."

"Did he mention a name?"

"I don't think so. I would've remembered if it was anybody local. Anybody local would've known there are better places to dive around here."

The boat rocked in the waves and I put a hand on the windshield to steady myself. "Which way does the current run here?"

He waved a hand toward the green mountains of St. Maarten.

"Where did you find his gear?"

Again, he waved toward the island. "About four hundred yards from here."

"I saw the stuff," I said. "Cribbs seems to think a shark did the damage."

"That's possible," he said. "They're around."

"Did you see one hanging around that day?"

"No, but that doesn't mean anything. I've seen them materalize like ghosts, out of nowhere."

"The cuts in the weight belt looked more like they'd been made by a knife—"

"That's possible, too. Anixter had a knife and he was out of air. The buckle on the belt was still fastened when I found it. Maybe it got stuck and he panicked and tried to cut it off. I've seen divers do screwier things in situations like that."

"He cut off his trunks, too?"

He said nothing to that, just shrugged.

"Was that his own equipment?"

"No. It was mine."

"How about his wife? Was she certified too?"

"No. She said she'd been down a couple of times, but didn't like it. She just went along for the ride."

"And she never left the boat the entire time you were under?"

"That's one thing I'm positive about."

"Did you see any other boats in the area?"

"Not that I remember."

"You say the current is strong here. Strong enough to carry a man to shore?"

I went on with the train of thought. "Say a diver had been dropped off here earlier. Would it have been possible for him to have been waiting down there without you seeing him?"

"Maybe, if he was careful, and didn't breathe a lot." His eyes widened as the idea crystalized in his mind. "You think that's what happened? You think somebody was waiting down there?"

"I'm just looking at all the possibilities."

"Then what happened to the body?"

"If there were signs of violence on it, knife wounds, for instance, they would have to keep it from being found," I speculated. "Who else knew where you were going to dive?"

"My partner, Sonny. But he had a group out that afternoon—"

"Don't worry, I don't consider him a suspect."

He shrugged. "As far as I know, only the four of us knew."

"How did Mrs. Anixter act when you told her you couldn't find her husband?"

He looked at me strangely. "That was something that always bothered me."

"Why?"

"When I came up with his equipment, she got hysterical. Cried and wailed all the way back to shore. She only stopped long enough to ask one question."

"What was that?"

"She wanted to know what the waiting period was before someone was declared legally dead."

The entire flight back to L.A. my thoughts drifted as unrelentingly toward the solution as that St. Maarten

137

current ran toward shore. No matter how hard I tried to swim in other directions, I wound up heading the same way.

It was almost ten in the evening when I pulled into my parking slot in front of my apartment, dog-tired and suffering from an intense case of heartburn from the catered cardboard the Eastern stewardess had jokingly referred to as "dinner." All I wanted was to make myself a strong drink and crawl into bed. I was definitely not in the mood for company; especially the two movie-extra heavies who detached themselves from the shadows and materialized on each side of my car.

They yanked open the doors and the one on the passenger's side stuck a .45 Browning automatic in my face. He was big and beefy and had a wide, loose face that gravity had gone to work on. The face didn't smile. "He'll drive," was all he said.

The one on the driver's side nudged me, and I moved over to keep from being sat on. They wedged me in firmly between them and the driver backed my car out of the driveway. The gun was jammed up under my rib cage, making it hard to breathe. The driver turned right onto Pacific and headed toward the Marina. He was slimmer than the other one, with a bony brow and a nose that someone had rearranged onto the side of his face, then decided it looked better where it had been, and moved it back again.

"Where are we going?" I asked, trying to sound calm. I wasn't calm. I was scared. Very scared. Nobody answered.

He got onto Washington. Longingly, I watched the tall, lighted office buildings of Marina del Rey passing outside the window. I thought about the couples and swinging singles out there in their favorite watering holes, drinking and dancing and performing their bird-like courtship rituals, trying to get the magic going for a night. They weren't exactly my kind of joints, but I wasn't so narrow-minded that I wasn't willing to bend a rule for an evening. "You guys want to pick up some chicks? I know a great place right over here—"

The gun barrel tried to find the seat behind my back and I sucked in some air and shut up. We got onto Lincoln and crossed Ballona Creek and the buildings were gone as we headed into the barren brown hills. The driver turned off onto a dirt road and we churned up dust for a short distance until he pulled up and stopped in front of a fence at the edge of the runway of a private industrial airport. They opened the doors and got out; the driver had a gun now too, a .38. "Out," the sagging-faced man said.

There were no stars, just a limitless blackness. The red lights bordering the runway blinked in sequence, away from us, beckoning planes from the dark and lonely sky.

"Okay," Saggy Face asked. "Who are you working for?"

"Truth, justice, and the American way," I said, I don't know why.

Nose Job stepped in fast and brought a hook from somewhere south of Tierra del Fuego that sent me to my knees, gasping for air like a sick guppy. He bent down and grabbed me under the arms, hoisted me up easily and leaned me against the car. Saggy Face leaned close, his breath hot and moist in my face. He was chewing a mint; I guess there's always something to be thankful for, if you just look for it.

He jammed his gun in my crotch. That didn't feel too good, either, but I couldn't work up enough breath to tell him. "Now listen, shit-for-brains," he said, "we can dance all night if you want, but we've all got better things to do, including you, I imagine. Now, I'm gonna ask you one more time: Who are you working for?"

I had to admit, he was a hell of a debater. "John Anixter," I gasped, barely.

He nodded and smiled and stepped back. He nodded at Nose Job, who put away his gun and grabbed my wrist before I had a chance to resist. He yanked my hand out and held it on the hood of my car while Saggy Face brought the barrel of the .45 down on it. I screamed as the pain shot halfway up my arm to my elbow, then I slid down the side of the car.

All I could do was cradle the hand and rock back and forth in the dirt as Saggy Face hovered over me and said: "The nuns used to do that to me in school when I did something I shouldn'ta. You been doing something you shouldn'ta, Asch. You been sticking your nose in other people's private business. I think we both know who I mean. Now if you keep it up, we're gonna have to come back and visit, and if we do, it ain't gonna be a slap on the wrist, it's gonna be traction-time. You get where I'm coming from?"

I might have said yes, I'm not sure. My hand felt as if it were full of broken glass.

"We'll leave your car back at your apartment," he said, and they got into the car and drove away, leaving me there.

I watched my taillights recede down the road and stood up. A cold, damp fog had begun to roll in from the ocean, chilling the sweat on my face and making me shiver. Maybe it would numb my swelling hand. I took a deep breath and started off. It was going to be a long, cold walk home, but I didn't mind. I kind of enjoyed being by myself.

I woke up groggy from the pain pills the E.R. doctor had given me. I also had a headache, which got worse when I reached up and smacked myself with the cast I'd forgotten about that was holding my two broken metacarpals in place. I swore and rubbed my head with my good hand, then got up and made coffee. I made extra noise doing that, thinking about how I owed those guys and how I would more than likely never get the chance to repay them.

After three cups, I'd cleared enough cobwebs to call Al. He had Phalen's arrest report. I thought about telling him about my dance partners last night, but rejected the idea. He would have just wanted me to waste a lot of time looking at mug shots, and I wasn't in the mood. It wouldn't have done any good, anyway. Even if I could have identified them, they would have had six witnesses who had been playing poker with them last night, my car was outside where they had thoughtfully dropped it, and there was no way to prove that my hand had not been stepped on when I'd bent down to pick up a quarter from the sidewalk. My blood pressure went up ten points when I thought about it, but I kept my mouth shut and took down what Al gave me.

Phalen had been arrested after the fire department had found evidence of arson in the grease fire that completely destroyed his Encino restaurant, Arnie's Greenhouse. Traces of accelerants, possibly gasoline, had been found in the kitchen area where the fire had started, but Phalen claimed that those were possibly cleaning solvents which had been kept in a closet there. The case was weak, but it had been filed, anyway.

I thanked Al and called a friend of mine at Hooper Holms. The Hooper Holms Casualty Index in Morristown, New Jersey, contains the names of more than six million individuals and lists their insurance histories. The purpose is to spot insurance fraud. They had Phalen's name. Before moving to California, Phalen had owned two buildings in Baltimore that had mysteriously gone up in flames. No legal charges had ever been brought against him in those cases and the insurance claims had been paid.

Arnie the Torch. With three fires to his credit in the past ten years, one more business going up in smoke would certainly bring him more heat than just the combustible kind. Maybe he figured it was time to humanize him claim base.

I called Anixter and gave him a report. When I told

him about my welcome home committee, he sounded shocked. "My God. Are you all right?"

"A broken hand. They were just administering an object lesson. They let me know that next time, the damage would be more extensive."

"You think they were working for this Phalen character?"

"Yeah, I think. And now he knows I'm working for you, not his wife."

"Have you told the police?"

"It wouldn't do any good—"

"But if he and Rhonda have been carrying on an affair all this time, and he's the kind of man you say he is, they could have plotted Chip's death from the beginning. He could have targeted Chip as a mark and sent her after him."

That thought had crossed my mind. Phalen certainly had the connections and the experience, and his mind seemed to run in those directions. "It's possible," I said, more to keep him from running off on that track than anything. "Did Chip own his own scuba gear, Mr. Anixter?"

"Huh? Yes."

"You're sure?"

"I should be. I paid enough for it. Why?"

I bypassed the question. "I'd like to put a twenty-four hour surveillance on both the woman and Phalen, Mr. Anixter, but that would run into some money—"

"I told you I don't care what it costs," he snapped.

My kind of client. I told him I'd keep in touch, then called Transcontinental Life. The agent handling the

Anixter claim was named Manning and I repeated what I'd learned to him, then asked if he could send an investigator over to Rhonda Anixter's apartment and on some pretext ask to see Chip's diving gear. When he asked what I was looking for, I told him I basically wanted an inventory of what was there. He said it should be no problem, and promised to get right on it.

I called some people I knew and arranged for round-the-clock surveillance on both Rhonda and Phalen, warning them to be careful, then called the phone company. I told the service rep that my name was Chip Anixter and that I'd just gotten my phone bill and noticed I'd been billed for a call to Fort Lauderdale I'd never made. I gave her Rhonda's number and she came back on the line and said she could find no record of any such call billed to that number. Indignantly, I asked what calls had been made in the past month that she *did* have a record for, and she read off a list. I took them down and hung up.

Out of the sixteen toll calls Rhonda had made, two were to a number in Yuma, Arizona, seven were to a number in Los Angeles, and four to a Hollywood number. I started dailing. The Hollywood number, as I suspected, was the Paradise; all the calls had been made since she had returned from the Caribbean. The Los Angeles number belonged to the law firm of Sadler, Bacon, and Pitts, Rhonda's attorneys. A woman named Zelda Banks answered the Yuma number when I called and it took a four-second scam to find out she was Rhonda's mother.

Manning called back after lunch. "There's nothing

there, he said. "She told my guy that she trashed the stuff after the accident. Too painful for her to keep, she said."

I couldn't help grinning.

"Another little item of note," he went on. "She's got a new attorney. A young, Beverly Hills fire-breather named Cohen. We've come up against him before in a couple of questionable fire claims. He's already talking a five-figure lawsuit for damages unless we can show good cause why her claim shouldn't be paid."

"When did this happen?"

"We were notified of the change of counsel this morning, right after I talked to you."

"How long would a lawsuit take to settle?"

"Months, years, who knows?"

"Tell them they're going to have to sue. Tell them there's new evidence to dispute the validity of the claim."

"But there isn't, really—"

"They don't know that. Besides, there might be, if we can drag this thing out."

"I don't know if the company will go for it—"

"Do what you can do."

He promised to try. I sat there, thinking about it, then went down to my car and drove downtown. Arnie Phalen's arson case was listed in the index of the Superior Court. I took down the number and gave it to the clerk, who came back with a file. There wasn't much in the file. The case had been dropped in preliminary for lack of evidence. Harold Cohen must have done a good job representing his client.

Phalen must have thought Rhonda's attorney was a little weak and put his own man in to push a little harder. I couldn't blame him, really; he was merely protecting his investment. Just as he had been protecting it when he'd sent his goons to break my hand.

There wasn't much to do now but wait, so I went home, took a pain pill, made myself a drink, and started.

The waiting ran into a week. Harold Cohen screamed and threatened, but Transcontinental stood firm. Phalen stayed away from Rhonda, but he visited Cohen's office twice during the week.

I was taking the Monday morning shift at Rhonda Anixter's apartment when the Porsche pulled out of the driveway and headed down the street. I put the glazed doughnut I was eating down on the front seat and followed her to I-10, where she headed east. She drove fast and it was hard to keep up in my old Dodge, but I managed to keep her in sight all the way to the Harbor freeway. She lost me there, but I had a pretty good idea where she was going. I confirmed it when I pulled up across from the Paradise and saw the Porsche parked in the lot.

Twenty minutes later, she came through the front door and headed to her car. She was wearing big sunglasses and had her hair up, but even without makeup she made me drool. It made me sad that this was as close as I would ever get to her, playing Peeping Tom, but then I guess we all have our roles to play in life. Maybe I should brown-nose the Director more. . . .

She turned right out of the driveway and headed toward Vermont, but two blocks up she suddenly pulled over to the curb, so I had to drive past her and park in the next block. I watched through my rear window as she got out of the Porsche and went to the curbside mailbox. Her body looked spectacular in a red tube top and tightfitting jeans, but my eyes were on the business-sized envelope she pulled out of her purse and dropped into the box.

She got back into her car and I waited until she had turned on Vermont before I got the fifteen colored blotters from the trunk of my car and walked back to the mailbox.

The pickup time marked on the box was 4:15, two hours away. I opened the mailbox, dropped in the blotters and went back to my car. I stopped at a nearby greasy spoon and killed some time downing a tuna fish sandwich and four cups of coffee, and was back at the mailbox by quarter to four.

The mail truck pulled up at 4:21, by my watch, but then my watch may have been a little fast. The mailman was opening the box when I trotted up, wearing my most worried expression. "Excuse me—"

He looked up, startled. "Huh?"

He was young, with shoulder-length dark hair and a beard. I hoped his attitude matched his appearance. What I needed was a little hang-loose flexibility, someone who would be willing to bend the rules a little to help out a fellow human being in distress.

I pointed up the street, and tried to put urgency in my voice. "I just live up the street here at 1015. I mailed a letter this afternoon and I'm sure I sent it to the wrong address. It's a check, and Jesus Christ, if it gets into the wrong hands and gets cashed, I'd be up shit's creek."

He shrugged. "I don't know what I can do about it—"

"If I could just take a look at the letter and see, I'd know whether to cancel the check or not—"

He frowned, his mouth following the lines of his mustache. "I can't go looking through all this mail—"

"You won't have to," I assured him. "After I mailed it and realized what I'd done, I took some blotters and dropped them in the box. The letter should be right below them."

He looked doubtful. "I don't know. . . ."

"Look, I don't have to touch anything. I know that's probably against the postal regulations. You can read me the address. I don't want the letter back or anything. I just want to know whether I should call the bank and cancel the check. I mean, if the check gets into the wrong hands, man, I'll really be screwed."

He bit his lip and made a sloughing motion with his shoulders. "I guess it'd be okay."

"I really appreciate this," I said truthfully.

The blotters were near the top of the pile of mail. He took the letter directly below them and picked it up, holding it away from me so I couldn't see it. "Charles Albertson?"

That was probably it. For some reason, they always seemed to use their own first names or the same initials.

The lack of imagination of the typical criminal mind never ceased to depress me. "That's the one."

"Two thirty-four Montvue Road," he read. "Old Towne, Montserrat."

"That takes a load off my mind, thanks," I said. "That's the right address." He handed me back my blotters and I thanked him again and jotted down the address in my notebook on the way to the car. I called my travel agent from a pay phone down the street and booked the first flight out of Miami, with connections to Antigua and Montserrat. Then I called Barbara Phalen and filled her in about her husband's affair with Rhonda Anixter. I figured I might as well have something nice to think about on the plane.

Montserrat was a green and rugged island paradise of forested mountains, manicured fields, and black sand beaches. Old Towne was a collection of affluent hillside houses overlooking a golf course and the sea. Two thirty-four Montvue was a pink house with a white shingle roof, surrounded by a white wrought iron fence festooned with flowers. I told my cab driver to wait for me and went up the walk to the front door.

The day was hot and sunny and the front door was wide open to let in the cool breeze that blew steadily from the ocean. I stepped inside and called out: "Hello?"

I heard his thongs slapping the tile floor before he appeared around the corner dressed in a pair of swim trunks. He had the unintelligent good looks and the lean, tanned body of a kid who surfed a lot and played volleyball on the beach and little else. His curly blond hair was wet.

"Hello, Chip." I looked around the place. It was light and airy, with whitewashed walls and rattan furniture. A swimming pool was visible out back through the open louvered doors. No wonder he needed money. "I can say one thing for you; you set yourself up well. What's the rent like?"

He stared at me, open-mouthed. The words were barely audible. "Who are you?"

"A detective hired by your father."

His expression turned to disgust and he threw both hands into the air and let them fall to his sides. "Shit. Dear old Dad. He even had to fuck this up—"

He was reverting to form—a whiner. "You're lucky he did. Rhonda had no intention of bringing that $300,000 to you. Why should she when she could have it all? You're legally dead and if you suddenly turned up alive, you'd be prosecuted for insurance fraud. By that time, she'd be long gone. She only agreed to send you money because she wanted to keep you placated and underground."

"How did you know about the money?" he asked, surprised.

"I got a look at the envelope it's being sent in. I knew that if the insurance settlement was held up long enough, you'd more than likely run out of money and have to send for some." I paused. I wanted to savor the look on his face when I told him. "She got it from Arnie Phalen."

His eyes widened. "Phalen?"

"He's in for a piece now. He found out what the scam was and cut himself in. She's even using his attorney. They've been having a good time together since you've been gone, by the way."

His hands clenched into fists and he stepped toward me. "You're a liar—"

I wasn't going to stand for any of that stuff; I figured I could handle him one-handed if I had to. I sidestepped him and put my good hand on his chest and shoved him back, hard. His foot hit the bottom of one of the rattan chairs and he lost his balance and sat down. I moved forward so that he couldn't get up without being hit. He didn't try.

"Don't be stupid," I said. "You were had, boy, from the moment she set her sights on you. Your old man was right. She was only after the money."

He stared up at me hatefully, like a beaten dog. "Shit."

"That's what you're in." I turned and started toward the door.

"Hey!" he shouted after me. "Where are you going?"

I stopped and turned around. "To find a beach somewhere. I've been in the Caribbean twice in a week, and I don't even have a tan."

He jumped up out of the chair and his hand jerked up. "Wait. What about me?"

I shrugged. "I was hired to find out what happened to you, not babysit. I don't think I'd care for that job." I held up my cast. "You're not my favorite person, boy. It's because of you I have this."

I started to go, then turned back.

"My advice to you would be to get your tail back to 'dear old Dad' as fast as you can and start doing some serious brown-nosing, because you're going to need his money to pay for your lawyer. If you lay it out for the insurance company now, you might just get off with probation."

I left him standing there and took the cab to the airport, where I called John Anixter. The phone connection was lousy, but it was good enough to get the message across. He sounded very happy at first to learn his son was alive, then he just got plain mad. He told me to "let the snot-nosed little sonofabitch find his own way back," and informed me I could expect a bonus when I got back.

I caught a LIAT puddle-jumper back to Antigua and checked into a quaint, two-hundred-year-old hotel in Nelson's dockyard on the isolated side of the island and spent the next four days soaking up some serious sun and a lot of rum punches and listening to the gentle lilt of steel bands. If there was trouble in paradise, it wasn't going to find me.

Bloody July

LOREN D. ESTLEMAN

"This one is special to me," Loren D. Estleman *writes about* "Bloody July." *"I have long wanted to incorporate elements of Detroit's Prohibition past into a contemporary story, and while it is a past the present city administration would rather pretend never happened, I contend that it is Detroit's violent history that has created its unique modern character. In addition, the personal element in this one parallels an incident in the history of my own family, which for the sake of delicacy and domestic tranquility I would rather not detail."*

Estleman *is a thirty-two-year-old newspaper reporter turned novelist. He lives in Whitmore Lake, Michigan, forty miles from Detroit where his detective Amos Walker works. The most recent of the Amos Walker novels is* Sugartown (1984).

THE HOUSE was a half-timbered Tudor job on Kendall, standing on four acres fenced in by a five-foot ornamental stone wall. It wasn't the only one in the area and looked as much like metropolitan Detroit as it tried to look like Elizabethan England. A bank of lilacs had been allowed to grow over the wall inside, obstructing the view of the house from the street, but from there inward the lawn was bare of foliage after the fashion of feudal estates to deny cover to intruders.

I wasn't one. As instructed previously, I stopped in front of the iron gate and got out to open it and was on my way back to the car when something black hurtled at me snarling out of the shrubbery. I clambered inside and shut the door and rolled up the window just as the thing leaped, scrabbling its claws on the roof and clouding the glass with its moist breath.

"Hector!"

At the sound of the harsh voice, the beast dropped to all fours and went on clearing its throat and glaring yellow at me through the window while a small man with a white goatee walked out through the gate and snapped a leash onto its collar. He wore a gray sport coat and no tie.

"It's all right, Walker," he said. "Hector behaves himself while I'm around. You are Amos Walker?"

I cranked the window down far enough to tell him I was, keeping my hand on the handle and my eye on the dog. "You're Mr. Blum?"

"Yeah. Drive on up to the house. I'll meet you there."

The driveway looped past an attached garage and a small front porch with carriage lamps mounted next to the door. I parked in front of the porch and leaned on the fender smoking a cigarette while Leonard Blum led the dog around back and then came through the house and opened the door for me. The wave of conditioned air hit me like a spray of cold water. It was the last day of June and the second of the first big heat wave of summer.

"You like dogs, Walker?"

"The little moppy noisy kind and the big gentle ones that lick your face."

"I like Dobermans. You can count on them to turn on you someday. With friends you never know." He ushered me into a dim living room crowded with heavy furniture and hung with paintings of square-riggers under full sail and bearded mariners in slick Sou'westers shouting into the bow wash. A varnished oak ship's wheel as big around as a hula hoop was mounted over the fireplace.

"Nautical, I know," said Blum. "I was in shipping a long time back. Never got my feet wet but I liked to pretend I was John Paul Jones. That wheel belonged to the *Henry Morgan*, fastest craft ever to sail the river. In my day, anyway."

"That doesn't sound like the name of an ore carrier."

"It wasn't."

I waited, but he didn't embroider. He was crowding eighty if it wasn't stuck to his heels already, with heavy black-rimmed glasses and a few white hairs combed diagonally across his scalp and white teeth that flashed too much in his beard to be his. There was a space there when we both seemed to realize we were being measured, and then he said:

"My lawyer gave me your name. Simon Weintraub. You flushed out an eyewitness to an accident last year that saved his client a bundle."

"I'm pretty good." I waited some more.

"How are you at tracing stolen property?"

"Depends on the property."

He produced a key from a steel case on his belt, hobbled over to a bare corner of the room, and inserted the key in a slot I hadn't noticed. The wood paneling opened in two sections, exposing a recessed rectangle tall enough for a man to stand in, lined in burgundy plush.

"Notice anything?" he asked.

"Looks like a hairdresser's casket."

"It's a gun cabinet. An empty gun cabinet. Three days ago there wasn't enough room to store another piece in it."

"Were you at home when it got empty?"

"My wife and I spent the weekend on Mackinac Island. I've got a place there. Whoever did it, it wasn't his first job. He cut the alarm wires and picked the locks to the front door and the cabinet slick as spit."

"What about Hector?"

"I put him in a kennel for the weekend."

"Are you sure someone didn't just have a key?"

"The only key to this cabinet is on my belt. It's never out of my sight."

"Who else lives here besides your wife?"

"No one. We don't have servants. Elizabeth's at her CPR class now. I've got a heart I wouldn't wish on an Arab," he added.

"What'd the police say?"

"I didn't call them."

I was starting to get the idea. "Have you got a list of the stolen guns?"

He drew two sheets folded lengthwise out of his inside breast pocket, holding them back when I reached for them. "When does client privilege start?"

"When I pick up the telephone and say hello."

He gave me the list. It was neatly typewritten, the firearms identified by make, caliber, patent dates, and serial number. Some handguns, four high-powered rifles, a few antiques, two shotguns. And a Thompson submachine gun. I asked him if he was a dealer.

"No, I'm in construction."

"Non-dealers are prohibited from owning automatic weapons," I said. "I guess you know that."

"I'd have gone to the cops if I'd wanted a lecture."

"Or a warrant for your arrest. Are any of these guns registered, Mr. Blum?"

"That's not a question you get to ask," he said.

I handed back the list. "So long, Mr. Blum. I've got some business up in Iroquois Heights, so I won't charge you for the visit."

"Wait, Walker."

I had my back to him when he said it. It was the way he said it that made me turn around. It didn't sound like the Leonard Blum I'd been talking to.

"Nothing in the collection is registered," he said. "The rifles and shotguns don't have to be, of course, and I just never got around to doing the paper on the handguns and the Thompson. I've never been fingerprinted."

"It's an experience no one should miss," I said.

"I'll take your word for it. Anyway, that's why I didn't holler cop. For a long time now I've lived for

157

that collection. My wife lays down for anything with a zipper; she's almost fifty years younger than me and it's no more than I have any right to expect. But pleasant memories are tied up with some of those pieces. I've seen what happens to old friends when they lose all interest, Walker. They wind up in wheelchairs stinking of urine and calling their daughters Charlie. I'd splatter my brains before I'd let that happen to me. Only now I don't have anything to do it with."

I got out one of my cards, scribbled a number on the back, and gave it to him. "Call this guy in Belleville. His name's Ben Perkins. He's a P.I. who doubles in apartment maintenance, which as lines of work go aren't so very different from each other. He's a cowboy, but a good one, which is what this job screams for. But I can't guarantee he'll touch it."

"I don't know." He was looking at the number. "Weintraub recommended you as the original clam."

"This guy makes me look like a set of those wind-up dime store dentures." I said so long again and let myself out, feeling cleansed. And as broke as a motel room chair.

The Iroquois Heights business had to do with a wandering wife I never found. What I did find was a deputy city prosecutor living off the town madam and a broken head courtesy of a local beat officer's monkey stick. The assistant chief is an old acquaintance. A week after the Kendall visit I was nursing my headache with aspirin and the office fan with pliers and a paper-clip when Lieutenant John Alderdyce of Detroit Homicide walked in. His black face glistened and he was breathing like a rhinoceros from the three-story climb. But his shirt and Chinese silk sport coat looked fresh. He saw what I was doing and said, "Why don't you pop for air conditioning?"

"Every time I get a fund started I get hungry." I laid down my tools and plugged in the fan. The blades turned, wrinkling the thick air. I lifted my eyebrows at John.

He drew a small white rectangle out of an inside pocket and laid it on my desk, lining up the edges with those of the blotter. It was one of my business cards. "These things turn up in the damnedest places," he said. "So do you."

"I'm paid to. The cards I raise as best I can and then send them out into the world. I can't answer for where they wind up."

He flipped it over with a finger. A telephone number was written on the back in a scrawl I recognized. I sighed and sat back.

"What'd he do," I asked, "hang himself or stick his tongue in a light socket?"

He jumped on it with both feet. "What makes it suicide?"

"Blum's wife was cheating on him, he said, and he lost his only other interest to a B-and-E. He as much as told me he'd take the back way out if that gun collection didn't find its way home."

"Maybe you better throw me the rest of it," he said.

I did, starting with my introduction to Blum's dog Hector and finishing with my exit from the house on Kendall. Alderdyce listened with his head down, stroking an unlit cigarette. We were coming up on the fifth anniversary of his first attempt to quit them.

"So you walked away from it," he said when I was through. "I never knew you to turn your back on a job just because it got too illegal."

I said, "We'll pass over that on account of we're so close. I didn't like Blum. When he couldn't bully me he tried wheedling and he caught me in the wrong mood. Was it suicide?"

"It plays that way. Wife came home from an overnight stay with one of her little bridge partners and found him shot through the heart with a .38 automatic. The gun was in his right hand and the paraffin test came up positive. Powder burns, the works. No note, but you can't have music too."

"Thirty-eight auto. You mean one of those Navy Supers?"

"Colt Sporting Pistol, Model 1902. It was discontinued in 1928. A real museum piece. The same gun was on a list we found in a desk drawer."

"I know the list. He said everything on it had been stolen."

"He lied. We turned your card in a wastebasket this morning. We tried to reach you."

"I was up in the Heights getting a lesson in police work, Warner Brothers style. Check out the wife's alibi?"

He nodded, rolling the cold cigarette along his lower lip. "A pro bowler in Harper Woods. You'd like him. Muscles on his elbows and if his I.Q. tests out at half his handicap you can have my pension. Blum started getting cold around midnight and she was at Fred Flintstone's place from ten o'clock on. She married Blum four years ago, about the time he turned seventy-five and turned over the operation of his construction firm to his partners. We're still digging."

"He told me he used to be in shipping." Alderdyce shrugged. I said, "I guess you called Perkins."

"The number you wrote on the card. Blum didn't score any more points with him than he did with you. I'm glad we never met. I wouldn't want to know someone who wasn't good enough for two P.I.'s with cardboard in their shoes."

I lit a Winston, just to make him squirm. "What I most enjoy paying rent on this office for is to provide a forum for overdressed fuzz to run down my profession. Self-snuffings don't usually make you this pleasant. Or is it the heat?"

"It's the heat," he said. "It's also this particular self-snuffing. Maybe I'm burning out. They say one good way of telling is when you find yourself wanting to stand the stiff on its feet and ask it a question."

"As for instance?"

"As for instance, 'Mr. Blum, would you please tell me why before you shot yourself you decided to shoot your dog?' "

I said nothing. After a little while he broke his

cigarette in two and flipped the pieces at my waste-basket and went out.

I finished my smoke, then broke out my Polk Administration Underwood and cranked a sheet into it and waited for my report to the husband of the runaway wife to fall into order. When I got tired of that I tore out the blank sheet and crumpled it and bonged it into the basket. My head said it was time to go home.

"Mr. Walker?"

I was busy locking the door to my private office. When I turned I was looking at a slender brunette of about thirty standing in the waiting room with the hall door closing on its pneumatic tube behind her. She wore her hair short and combed almost over one eye and had on a tailored black jacket that ran out of material just below her elbows, on top of a ruffled white blouse and a tight skirt to match the jacket. Black purse and shoes. The weather was too hot for black, but she made it look cool.

I got my hat off the back of my head and said I was Walker.

She said, "I'm Andrea Blum. Leonard Blum is—was my husband."

I unlocked my door again and held it for her. Inside the brain room she glanced casually at the butterfly wallpaper and framed *Casablanca* poster and accepted the chair I held for her, the one whose legs were all the same length. I sat down behind the desk and said I was sorry about Mr. Blum.

She smiled slightly. "I won't pretend I'm destroyed. It's no secret our marriage was a joke. But you get used to having someone around, and then when he's not—" She spread her hands. "Leonard told me he tried to hire you to trace his stolen guns and that you turned him down."

"I'd have had to tell the police that a cache of unregistered firearms was loose," I said. "Three out of five people in this town carry guns. They'd like to keep the other two virgin."

"Don't explain. I was just as happy they were taken. Guns frighten me. Anyway, that's not why I'm here. The police think Leonard's death was self-inflicted."

"You don't."

She moved her head. The sunlight caught a reddish thread in her black hair. "The burglary infuriated him. After that other detective refused to take the case he was determined to find one that would. He was ready to do it himself if it came to that. Do people shoot themselves when they're angry, Mr. Walker?"

"Never having shot myself I can't say."

"And he wouldn't have killed Hector," she went on. "He loved that dog. Besides, where could he have gotten the gun? It was one of those missing."

"Could be the burglars overlooked it and he just didn't tell you. And it wouldn't be the first time a suicide took something he loved with him. Generally it's the wife. You're lucky, Mrs. Blum."

"That he cared less for me than he did for his dog? I deserve that, I guess. Marrying an old man for his money gets boring. All those other men were just a diversion. I loved Leonard in my way." She lined up her fingers primly on the purse in her lap. The nails were sharp and buffed to a high gloss, no polish. "He didn't kill himself. Whoever killed him shot the dog first when it came at him."

I offered her a cigarette from the deck. When she shook her head I lit one for myself and said, "I've got a question, but I don't want one of those nails in my eye."

"Insurance," she said. "A hundred thousand dollars, and I'm the sole beneficiary. It's worth more than twice the estate minus debts outstanding. And yes, if suicide is established as cause of death the policy is void. But that's only part of why I'm here, though I admit it's the biggest part. At the very least I owe it to Leonard to find out who murdered him."

"Who do you suspect?"

"I can't think of anyone. We seldom had visitors. He outlived most of his friends and the only contact he had with his business partners was over the telephone. He was in semi-retirement."

She gave me the name of the firm and the partners' names. I wrote them down. "What did your husband do before he went into construction?" I asked.

"He would never tell me. Whenever I asked he'd say it didn't matter, those were dead days. I gather it had something to do with the river but he never struck me as the sailor type. May could tell you. His first wife. May Shinstone, her name is now. She lives in Birmingham."

I wrote that down too. "I'll look into it, Mrs. Blum. Until the cops stop thinking suicide, anyway. They frown on competition. Meanwhile I think you should find another place to stay."

"Why?"

"Because if Mr. Blum was murdered odds are it was by the same person who stole his guns, and that person sneezes at locks. If you get killed I won't have anyone to report to."

After a moment she nodded. "I have a place to stay."

I believed her

After she left, poorer by a check in the amount of my standard three-day retainer, I called Ben Perkins. We swapped insults and then I drew on a favor he owed me and got the number of a gun broker downtown, one who wasn't listed under Guns in the Yellow Pages. Breaking the connection I could almost smell one of the cork-tipped ropes Perkins smoked. When he lit one up in your presence you wouldn't have to see him pull it out of his boot to know where he kept them.

Eleven rings in, a voice with a Mississippi twang came on and recited the number I had just dialed.

"I'm a P.I. named Walker," I said. "Ben Perkins gave me your number."

He got my number and said he'd call back. We hung up.

Three minutes later the telephone rang. It was Mississippi. "Okay, Perk says you're cool. What?"

"I need a line on some hot guns," I said.

"Nix, not over the squawker. What's the tag?"

"Fifty, if you've got what I want."

"Man, I keep a roll of fifties in the crapper. Case I run out of Charmin, you know? A hunnert up front. No refunds."

"Sixty-five. Fifty up front. Nothing if I don't come away happy."

"Sevenny-five and no guarantees. Phone's gettin' *heavy*, man."

I said okay. We compared meeting places, settling finally on a city parking lot on West Lafayette at six o'clock.

My next call was to Leonard Blum's construction firm, where a junior partner referred me to Ed Klagan at a building site on Third. Klagan's was one of the names Andrea Blum had given me. I asked for the number at the building site.

"There aren't any phones on the twenty-first floor, mister," the junior partner told me.

An M. Shinstone was listed in Birmingham. I tried the number and cradled the receiver after twenty rings. It was getting slippery. I got up, peeling my shirt away from my back, stood in front of the clanking fan for a minute, then hooked up my hat and jacket. The thermometer at the bank where I cashed Mrs. Blum's check read eighty-seven, which was as cool as it had been all day.

It was hotter on Third Street. The naked girders straining up from the construction site were losing their vertical hold in the smog and twisting heat waves, and the security guard at the opening in the board fence had sweated through his light blue uniform shirt. I shouted my business over the clattering pneumatic hammers. At length he signaled to a broad party in a hardhat and necktie who was squinting at a blueprint in the hands of a glistening, half-naked black man. The broad party came over, getting bigger as he approached until I was looking up at the three chins folded over his Adam's apple. The guard left us.

"Mr. Klagan?"

"Yeah. You from the city?"

"The country, originally." I showed him my I.D. "Andrea Blum hired me to look into her husband's death."

"I heard he croaked himself."

"That's what I'm being paid to find out. What was his interest in the construction firm?"

"Strictly financial. Pumped most of his profits back into the business and arranged an occasional loan when we were on the shorts, which wasn't often. He put together a good organization. Look, I got to get back up top. The higher these guys go the slower they work. And the foreman's a drunk."

"Why don't you fire him?"

He uncovered tobacco-stained teeth in a sour grin. "Local 226. Socialism's got us by the uppers, brother."

"One more question. Blum's life before he got into construction is starting to look like a mystery. I thought you could clear it up."

"Not me. My old man might. They started the firm together."

"Where can I find him?"

"Mount Elliott. But you better bring a shovel."

"I was afraid it'd be something like that," I said.

"All I know is Blum came up to the old man in January of '34 with a roll of greenbacks the size of a coconut and told him he looked too smart to die a foreman. He had the bucks, Pop had the know-how."

He showed me an acre of palm and moved off. I smoked a cigarette to soothe a throat made raw by yelling over the noise and watched him mount the hydraulic platform that would take him up to the unfinished twenty-first floor. Thinking.

The parking lot on West Lafayette was in the shadow of the *News* building; stepping into it from the heat of the street was like falling headfirst into a pond. I stood in the aisle, mopping the back of my neck with my soaked handkerchief and looking around. My watch read six on the nose.

A horn beeped. I looked in that direction. The only vehicle occupied was a ten-year-old Dodge club cab pickup parked next to the building with Michigan cancer eating through its rear fenders and a dull green finish worn down to brown primer in leprous patches. I went over there.

The window on the driver's side came down, leaking loud music and framing a narrow, heavy-lidded black face in the opening. "You a P.I. named Walker?"

I said I was. He reached acrosss the interior and popped up the lock button on the passenger's side. The cab was paved with maroon plush inside and had an instrument-studded leather dash and speakers for a sound system that had cost at least as much as the book on the pickup, pouring out drums and electric guitars at brain-throbbing volume. He'd had the air conditioner on recently and it was ten degrees cooler inside.

My eardrums had been raped enough for one day. I shouted to him to turn down the roar. He twirled a knob and then it was just us and the engine ticking as it cooled.

My host was a loose tube of bones in a red tank top and blue running shorts. And alligator shoes on his bare feet. He caught me looking at them and said, "I got an allergy to everything but lizard. You carrying?"

When I hesitated he showed me the muzzle of a nickel-plated .357 magnum under the magazine he had lying face down on his lap. I didn't think he was the *Ebony* type. I took the Smith & Wesson out of its belt holster slowly and handed it to him butt first. His lip curled.

"Police Special. Who you, Dick Tracy? I got what you want here." He laid my revolver on his side of the dash and snaked an arm over the back of the seat into the compartment behind. After some rummaging he came up with a chromed Colt Python as long as my forearm. "Man, you plug them with this mother, the lead goes through them, knocks down a light pole across the street."

"I've got no beef with Detroit Edison."

He dropped his baggy grin, put the big magnum back behind the seat and its little brother on the dash next to my .38, and held out his palm. I laid seventy-five dollars in it. He folded the bills and slid them under a clip on the sun visor. "You after hot iron."

"Just its history." I recited Blum's list so far as I remembered it. "They came up gone from a house on Kendall a little over a week ago," I added. "Unless someone's hugging the ground they should be on the market by now. Some of those pieces are pretty rare. You'd know them."

"Ain't come my way. I can let you have a .45 auto Army, never issued. Two hunnert."

"How many notches?"

"Man, this is a virgin piece. The barrel, anyway."

"The guns," I said. "You'd hear if they were available. It's a lot of iron to hit the street all at one time."

"When S & W talks, people listen. Only I guess it missed me."

"Okay, hang your ears out. I've got another seventy-five says they'll show up soon." I gave him my card.

"Last week a fourteen-year-old kid give me that much for a Saturday night banger I don't want to be in the same building with when it goes off. Listen, I can put you behind a Thompson Model 1921 for a thousand. The Gun That Won Chicago. Throw in a fifty-round drum."

I looked back at him with my hand on the door handle. I'd clean forgotten that item on Blum's list. "You've got a Thompson?"

His eyes hooded over. "Could be I know where one can be got."

I peeled three fifties off the roll in my pocket and held them up.

"I trade you a thousand-dollar piece for a bill and a half? Get out of my face, turkey white meat." He turned on the sound system. The pickup's frame buzzed.

"Ooh, jive," I said, turning it off. "You keep the gun. All I want is the seller's name. There's a murder involved."

He hesitated. I skinned off another fifty. He put his fingers on them. I held on.

"I call you, man," he said.

I tore the bills in two and gave him half. "You know the speech."

"Ain't no way to treat President Grant." But he clipped the torn bills with the rest and gave me back my gun, tipping out the cartridges first. There's no more trust in the world.

Shadows were lengthening downtown, cooling the pavement without actually lowering the temperature. I caught a sandwich and a cold beer at a counter and used the pay telephone to try the Birmingham number again. A husky female voice answered.

"May Shinstone?"

"Yes?"

I told her who I was and what I was after. There was a short silence before she said, "Leonard's dead?"

I made a face at the snarl of penciled numbers on the wall next to the telephone. "I'm sorry, Mrs. Shinstone. I got so used to it I forgot everyone didn't know."

"Don't apologize. It was just a surprise. It's been two years since I've seen Leonard, and almost that long since I've thought about him. I don't know how I can help you."

"Just now I'm sweeping up whatever's lying around. I'll sort it out later. I need some stuff on his life before January 1934."

"That isn't a story for the telephone, Mr. Walker."

There was something in her tone. I played around with it for a second, then poked it into a drawer. "If you have a few minutes this evening I'd like to come talk to you about it," I said.

"How big is your car trunk?"

"Would you say that again, Mrs. Shinstone? We have a bad connection."

"I'm giving up the house here and moving to an apartment in Royal Oak. I have one or two things left to move. If your trunk's big enough I can dismiss the cab I have waiting." She gave me her address.

I said, "I'll put the spare tire in the back seat."

I paused with my hand on the receiver, then unhooked it again and used another quarter to call my service. Lieutenant Alderdyce had tried to reach me and wanted me to call him back. I dialed his extension at Headquarters.

"I spoke to Mrs. Blum a little while ago," he said. "You're fired."

"Funny, you don't sound like her."

"She'll tell you the same thing. Blum's death is starting not to look like suicide and that means you can go back to your bench and leave the field to the first string."

"How much not like suicide is it starting to look?"

"Just for the hell of it we ran Blum's prints. We got a positive."

"He told me he'd never been printed."

"He must've forgot," Alderdyce said. "We didn't mess with the FBI. They destroy their records once a subject turns seventy. We got a match in a box of stuff on its way to the incinerator because it was too old to bother feeding into the computer. There is no Leonard Blum. But Leo Goldblum got to know these halls during Prohibition, whenever the old racket squad found it prudent to round up the Purple Gang and ask questions."

"Blum was a Purple?"

"Nice Jewish boys, those. When they weren't gunning each other down and commuting to Chicago to pull off the St. Valentine's Day Massacre for Capone they found time to ship bootleg hootch across the river from Canada. That was Goldblum's specialty. He was arrested twice for transporting liquor from the Ecorse docks and drew a year's probation in '29 on a Sullivan rap. Had a revolver in his pocket."

"Explains why he never registered his guns," I said. Licenses aren't issued to convicted felons. "That was a long time ago, John."

"Yeah, well, there's something else. Ever hear of Bloody July?"

"Sounds like the name of a punk rock group. No, wasn't that when they killed Jerry Buckley?"

"The golden boy of radio. Changed his stand on the mayor's recall on July 22, 1930, and a few hours later three Purples left him in a pool of blood in the lobby of the Hotel LaSalle. And during the first two weeks of the month the gang got frisky and put holes in ten of their mob playmates. It was a good month not to be a cop."

"All this history is leading someplace, I guess."

"Yeah. We got a lot of eager young uniforms here. One of them spent a couple of hours after his shift was over pawing through dusty records in the basement and matched the bullet that killed Blum with the ballistics report on the shooting of one Emmanuel Eckleberg, D.O.A. at St. Mary's Hospital July 6, 1930."

"Yesterday was July sixth," I said. "You're telling me someone waited all these years to avenge Manny Whatsizname on the anniversary of his death with the same gun that was used to kill him?"

"Eckleberg. You want someone to tell you that, call Hollywood. I just read you what we've got. You're walking, right?"

"Give me some time to square away a couple of things for my report."

He might have said "Uh-oh." I can't be sure because I was hanging up. It was getting to be a hell of a case, all right.

———

The address I wanted in Birmingham belonged to a small crackerbox with blue aluminum siding and a rosebush that had outgrown its bed under the picture window. My watch read seven-thirty and the sky showed no signs of darkening. You get a lot more for your money by hiring a private investigator in the summertime.

My knock was answered by a tall slim woman in sweats with blond streaks in her gray hair drawn up under a knotted handkerchief. She had taken the time to put on lipstick and rub rouge into her cheeks, but she really didn't need it. She had to be in her early seventies but looked twenty years younger. Her eyes were flat blue.

She smiled. "You look like you were expecting granny glasses and a ball of yarn."

"I was sort of looking forward to it," I said, taking off my hat. "No one seems to knit any more except football players."

"I never could get the knack. Come in."

The place looked bigger inside, mainly because there was hardly any furniture in it and the walls and floor were bare. She led me to a heavy oak table with the round top removed and leaning against the pedestal base. "Will it fit?" she asked.

"Search me. I flunked physics." I put my hat back on and got to work.

It was awkward, but the top eventually slid onto the ledge where the spare belonged and the pedestal fit diagonally into the well. She carried out a carton of books and slid it onto the back seat. "Take Telegraph down to Twelve Mile," she said, getting in on the passenger's side in front.

On the road I asked if Mr. Shinstone was waiting for her in Royal Oak.

"He died in '78. I would have sold the place then, but my sister got sick and I took her in. She passed away six weeks ago."

I said I was sorry. She shrugged. "You were married to Leonard Blum when he was Leo Goldblum?" I asked.

She looked at me, then untied her handkerchief and shook her hair loose. She kept it short. "You've been doing your homework. Have you got a cigarette?"

I got two out, lit them from the dash lighter, and gave her one. She blew smoke into the slipstream outside her window. "I started seeing him when I was in high school," she said. "He was twenty and very dashing. They all were; handsome boys in sharp suits and shiny new automobiles. We thought they were Robin Hoods. Never mind that people got killed, it was all for a good cause. The right to get hung over. The world was different then."

"Just the suits and automobiles," I put in. "Prohibition was repealed in December 1933. In January 1934, Goldblum shortened his name and invested his bootlegging profits in construction."

"He and Ed Klagan, Sr. had a previous understanding. I don't know how many buildings downtown are still being held up by people Leo didn't get on with. Mind you, I only suspected these things at the time."

"Was Manny Eckleberg one of them?"

"Who was he?"

I told her as much as I knew. We were stopped at a light and I was watching her. She was studying the horizontal suburban scenery. "I think I remember it. It was during that terrible July. Leo and some others were questioned by the police. Somebody was convicted for it. Abe Somebody; my sister dated him once or twice. Leo and I were married soon after and I remember hoping it wouldn't mean a postponement."

"Why was he killed?"

"A territorial dispute, I supose. It was a long time ago."

"Did you divorce Blum because of his past?"

"I could say that and sound noble. But I just got tired of being married to him. That was twenty years ago and he was already turning into an old crab. From what I saw of him during the times I ran into him since I'd say he never changed. Turn right here."

She had three rooms and a bath in the back half of a house on Farnum. I carried the table inside and set both pieces down in the middle of a room full of cartons and furniture. She added the box of books to the pile. "Thank you, Mr. Walker. You're a nice man."

"Mrs. Shinstone," I said, "Can you tell me why Blum might have been killed by the same gun that killed Manny Eckleberg?"

"Heavens, no. You said he was killed by a gun from his collection, didn't you?" I nodded. "Well. I guess that tells us something about the original murder then, doesn't it? Not that it matters."

She let me use her telephone to call my service. I had a mesage. I asked the girl from whom.

"He wouldn't leave his name, just his number." She gave it to me. I recognized it.

This time it rang fourteen times before the voice came on. "What've you got for me, Mississippi?" I asked.

"They's a parking lot on Livernois at Fort," he said.

"Good view of the river."

"No more parking lots. Let's make it my building in half an hour."

I broke the connection, thanked Mrs. Shinstone, and got out of her new living room.

The sky was purpling finally when I stepped into the foyer of my office building. A breeze had come up to peel away the smog and humidity. I mounted the stairs, stopping when something stiff prodded my lower back.

"Turn around, turkey white meat."

The something stiff was withdrawn and I obeyed. The lanky gun broker had stepped out from behind the propped-open fire door and was standing at the base of the stairs in his summer running outfit and alligator shoes. His right hand was wrapped around the butt of a lean automatic.

"Bang, you dead." He flashed a grin and reversed the gun, extending the checked grip. "Go on, see how she feels. Luger. Ninety bucks."

I said, "That's not a Luger. It's a P-38."

"Okay, eighty-five. 'Cause you discerning."

"Keep the gun. I'm getting my fill of them." I produced my half of the two hundred I'd torn earlier, holding it back when he reached for it.

He moved a shoulder and clipped the pistol under his tank top. "He goes by Shoe. I don't know his right name. White dude, big nose. When he turns sideways everything disappears but that beak. Tried to sell me the tommy gun and some other stuff on your list. Told him I had to scratch up cash. He says call him here." He handed me a fold of paper from the pocket of his shorts. "Belongs to a roach hatchery at Wilson and Webb."

"This better be the square." I gave him the abbreviated currency.

"Hey, I deal hot merchandise. I got to be honest."

They had just missed the hotel putting through the John Lodge and that was too bad. It was eight stories of charred brick held together with scaffolding and pigeon splatter. An electric sign ran up the front reading   O L PON   C. After five minutes I gave up wondering what it was trying to say and went inside. A kid in an Afro and army BVD undershirt looked up from the copy of *Bronze Thrills* he was reading behind the desk as I approached. I said, "I'm looking for a white guy named Shoe. Skinny guy with a big nose. He lives here."

"If his name ain't Smith or Jones it ain't in the register." He laid a dirty hand on the desk, palm up.

I rang the bell on the desk with his head and repeated what I'd said.

"Twenty-three," he groaned, rubbing his forehead. "Second floor, end of the hall."

It had been an elegant hall, with thick carpeting and wainscoting to absorb noise, but the floorboards whimpered now under the shiny carpet and the plaster bulged over the dull oak. I rapped on twenty-three. The door opened four inches and I was looking at a smoky brown eye and a nose the size of my fist.

"I'm the new house man," I said. "We got a complaint you've been playing your TV too loud."

"Ain't got a TV." He had a voice like a pencil sharpener.

"Your radio, then."

The door started to close. I leaned a shoulder against it. When it sprang open I had to change my footing to keep my face off the floor. He was holding a short-barreled revolver at belly level.

A day like this brought a whole new meaning to the phrase "Detroit iron."

"You're the dick, let's see your I.D."

I held it up.

"Okay. I'm checking out tonight anyway." The door closed.

I waited until the lock snapped, then walked back downstairs, making plenty of noise. I could afford to. I'd had a good look at Shoe and at an airline ticket folder lying on the lamp table next to the door.

I passed the reader in the lobby without comment

and got into my crate parked across the street in front of a mailbox. While I was watching the entrance and smoking a cigarette, a car parked behind mine and a fat woman in a green dress levered herself out to mail a letter and scowl at me through the windshield. I smiled back.

The streetlights had just sprung on when Shoe came out lugging two big suitcases and turned into the parking lot next door. Five minutes later a blue Plymouth with a smashed fender pulled out of the lot and the light fluttered on a big-nosed profile. I gave him a block before following.

We took the Lodge down to Grand River and turned right onto Selden. After three blocks the Plymouth slid into a vacant space just as a station wagon was leaving it. I cruised on past and stopped at the next intersection, adjusting my rearview mirror to watch Shoe angle across the street on foot, using both hands on the bigger of the two suitcases. He had to set it down to open a lighted glass door stenciled ZOLO-TOW SECURITIES, then brace the door with a foot while he backed in towing his burden.

I found a space around the corner and walked back. Two doors down I leaned against the closed entrance to an insurance office, fired a Winston, and chased mosquitoes with the glowing tip while Shoe was busy striking a deal with the pawnbroker.

He was plenty scared, all right.

It was waiting time, the kind you measure in ashes. I was on my third smoke when a blue-and-white cut into the curb in front of Zolotow's and a uniform with a droopy gunfighter's moustache got out from behind the wheel.

The glass door opened just as the cop had both feet on the pavement. He drew his side arm and threw both hands across the roof of the prowl car. "Freeze! Police!"

Empty-handed, Shoe backpedaled. The cop yelled freeze again, but he was already back inside. The door drifted shut. A second blue-and-white wheeled into the block, and then I heard sirens.

A minute crawled past. I counted four guns trained on the door. Blue and red flashers washed the street in pulsating light. Then the door flew open again and Shoe was on the threshold cradling a Chicago typewriter.

Someone hollered, "Drop it!"

Thompsons pull to the left and up. The muzzle splattred fire, its bullets sparking off the first prowl car's roof, pounding dust out of the granite wall across the street and shattering windows higher up, tok-tok-tok-tok-tok.

The return shots came so close together they made one long roar. Shoe slammed back against the door and slid into a sitting position spraddle-legged in the entrance, the submachine gun in his lap.

As the uniforms came forward, guns out, an unmarked unit fishtailed into the street. Lieutenant Alderdyce was out the passenger's side while it was still rocking on its springs. He glanced down at the body on the sidewalk, then looked up and spotted me in the crowd of officers. "What the hell are you doing here?"

"Mainly abusing my lungs," I said. "How about you?"

"Pawnbroker matched the guns this clown was selling to the hot sheet. He made an excuse and called us from the back."

I said, "He was running scared. He had an airline ticket and he checked out of the hotel where he was living. He was after a getaway stake."

"The murder hit the radio tonight. When his suicide scam went bust he rabbited."

The plainclothes man who had come with Alderdyce leaned out the open door of the pawnshop. Shoe was acting as a doorstop now. "He had all the handguns in the suitcase except one or two, John."

"Hey, this guy's still alive."

Everyone looked at the uniform down on one knee beside Shoe. The wounded man's chest rose and fell feebly beneath his bloody shirt. Alderdyce leaned forward.

"It's over," he said. "No sense lying your way deeper into hell. Why'd you kill Blum?"

Shoe looked up at him. His eyes were growing soft. After a moment his lips moved. On that street with the windows going up on both sides and police radios squawking it got very quiet.

It was even quieter on Farnum in Royal Oak, where night lay warm on the lawns and sidewalks and I towed a little space of silence through ratching crickets on my way to the back door of the duplex. The lights were off inside. I rang the bell and had time to smoke a cigarette between the time they came on and when May Shinstone looked at me through the window. A moment later she opened the door. Her hair was tousled and she had on a blue robe over a lighter blue nightgown that covered her feet. Without makeup she looked older, but still nowhere near her true age.

"Isn't it a little late for visiting, Mr. Walker?"

"It's going to be a busy night," I said. "The cops will be here as soon as they find out you've left the place in Birmingham and get a change of address."

"I don't know what you're talking about, but come in. When I was young we believed the night air was bad for you."

She closed the door behind me. The living room looked like a living room now. The cartons were gone and the books were in place on the shelves. I said, "You've been busy."

"Yes. Isn't it awful? I'm one of those compulsive people who can't go to sleep when there's a mess to be cleaned up."

"You can't have gotten much sleep lately, then. Leaving Shoe with all those guns made a big mess."

"Shoe? I don't—"

"The cops shot him at the place where he tried to lay them off. When he found out he was mixed up in murder he panicked. He made a dying statement in front of seven witnesses."

She was going to brazen it out. She stood with her

back to the door and her hands in the pockets of her robe and a marble look on her face. Then it crumbled. I watched her grow old.

"I let him keep most of what he stole," she said. "It was his payment for agreeing to burgle Leo's house. All I wanted was the Colt automatic, the .38 he used to kill Manny Eckleberg. Shoe—his name was Henry Schumacher—was my gardener in Birmingham. I hired him knowing of his prison record for breaking and entering. I didn't dream I'd ever have use for his talents in that area."

"You had him steal the entire collection to keep Blum from suspecting what you had in mind. Then on the anniversary of Eckleberg's murder you went back and killed him with the same gun. Pure poetry."

"I went there to kill him, yes. He let me in and when I pointed the gun he laughed at me and tried to take it away. We struggled. It went off. I don't expect you to believe that."

"It doesn't matter what I believe because it stinks first-degree any way you smell it," I said. "So you stuck his finger in the trigger afterwards and fired the gun through the window or something to satisfy the paraffin test and make it look like suicide. Why'd you kill the dog?"

"After letting me in, Leo set it loose in the grounds. It wouldn't let me out the door. I guess he'd trained it to trap intruders until he called it off. So I went back and got the gun and shot it. That hurt me more than killing Leo, can you imagine that? A poor dumb beast."

"What was Manny Eckleberg to you?"

"Nothing. I never knew him. He was just a small-time bootlegger from St. Louis who thought he could play with the Purple Gang."

I said nothing. Waiting. After a moment she crossed in front of me, opened a drawer in a bureau that was holding up a china lamp, and handed me a bundle of yellowed envelopes bound with a faded brown ribbon.

"Those are letters my sister received from Abe Steinmetz when he was serving time in Jackson prison for Eckleberg's murder," she said. "In them he explains how Leo Goldblum paid him to confess to the murder. He promised him he wouldn't serve more than two years and that there would be lots more waiting when he got out. Only he never got out. He was stabbed to death in a mess room brawl six months before his parole.

"I was the one who was dating Abe, Mr. Walker; not my sister. I was seeing him at the same time I was seeing Leo. He swore her to secrecy in the letters, believing I wouldn't understand until he could explain things in person. The money would start our marriage off right, he said. But instead of waiting I married Leo."

She wet her lips. I lit a Winston and gave it to her. She inhaled deeply, her fingers fidgeting and dropping ash on the carpet. "My sister kept the secret all these years. It wasn't until she died and I opened her safety deposit box and read the letters—" She broke off and mashed out the cigarette in a copper ashtray atop the bureau. "Do I have time to get dressed and put on lipstick before the police arrive? They never even gave

Leo time to grab a necktie whenever they took him in for questioning."

I told her to take as much time as she needed. At the bedroom door she paused. "I don't regret it, you know. Maybe I wouldn't have been happy married to Abe. But when I think of all those wasted years—well, I don't regret it." She went through the door.

Waiting, I pocketed the letters, shook the last cigarette out of my pack, and struck a match. I stared at the flame until it burned down to my fingers.

He had all the handguns in the suitcase except one or two.

I dropped the match and vaulted to the bedroom door. Moving too damn slowly. I had my hand on the knob when I heard the shot.

The temperatures soared later in the month, and with them the crime statistics. The weatherman called it the hottest July on record. The newspapers had another name for it, but it had already been used.

Say a Prayer
for the Guy

NELSON ALGREN

Though he never wrote mystery stories, Nelson Algren shared with hard–boiled detective writers a fascination for the inhabitants of the backstreets. His ability to understand his grotesque characters allowed him to sympathize without sentimentalizing them. "Say a Prayer for the Guy" combines two of his favorite subjects—saloons and poker. This uncollected story first appeared in 1958—nine years after The Man with the Golden Arm.

Nelson Algren died in 1981 at the age of seventy-nine.

THAT GAME began as it always began, the drinkers drank what they always drank. The talkers said what they always said, "Keep a seat open for Joe."

Frank, John, Pete, and I, each thinking tonight might be the night he'd win back all he'd lost last week to Joe. Yes, and perhaps a little more.

Joe, poor old Joe, all his joys but three have been taken away. To count his money, play stud poker, then secretly to count it once more—and the last count always the best—that there is more there than before is no secret.

Joe, old Joe, with his wallet fat as sausage and his money green as leaves. Who needs sports, cats, them like that? That call for mixed drinks and blame God if they've mixed too much? Who needs heavy spenders, loudmouth hollerers, them like *that*? Drinking is to make the head heavy, not the tongue loose. Drinking is for when nobody shows up to play poker. You want to make the feet light? Go dancing. Dance all night.

"Here come Joe," Phil, the bartender, told us, and sure enough, here he came. With his wallet full.

"Joe, you don't look so good," John told him as soon as he sat down, "you look so *peckid*."

"I don't feel so good," the old man told us, "I *feel* peckid."

"You feel peckid, take it easy," advised Frank.

I put a dime in the juke, all on Perry Como. I don't care what Perry sings, so long as he sings. The box coughed once and gave me back my dime. It doesn't like Perry. Well, it was my dime. I put it right back. *I* like Perry.

This time it didn't cough. It picked Elvis Presley singing *All Shook Up*. I got nothing against Elvis. It was just that it was my dime.

But that Frank began humming and shaking along with the song as if it had been his money.

Then the game went as it always went, the drinkers drank what they always drank, the talkers said what they always said, "Looks like Joe's night again."

Yet, just as Joe reached for the deck, as the juke cried out *I Need Your Love*, everything went strange.

The juke coughed on a note, and went on coughing, how it does when someone leans against it. I saw Joe's hands shuffling, but he shuffled too slow. A red deuce twisted out of the deck and dropped to the floor like a splash of blood. Joe fell forward onto the table, without a gasp, without a sound.

Up jumped Frank, the first to realize. "Joe! Wake up!" He seized Joe's wrists and began massaging them. I opened the old man's collar and his head flopped like a rooster's. O, I didn't like the looks of things in the least. Now I wanted the juke to play *anything*.

"*Please* wake up," Frank pleaded. "Old friend! My one true friend!"

But his one true friend didn't hear.

So we lifted Joe, old Joe, onto the long glass of the shuffleboard. We lay him down gently under the lights that say GAME COMPLETED. Frank began to massage his heart.

"I saw something wrong the second he sat down," John boasted. "I told him."

"Now you look a little peckid yourself," I told him. He didn't like that.

"You typewriter pounder," he told me, "how some day *you* look," and drew back his lips in a grin almost as bad as Joe's.

"How *you* look, too, someday, old dummy John,"

little Pete suddenly took my part, and stretched his mouth back and made a horrible face, so that he looked even worse than Joe. Then he ducked under the table to gather the cards.

"Give up," I told Frank, "if he comes to now, he'd be an idiot the rest of his days. When the breath stops the brain starts to melt, right that same second." It was something I'd read somewhere.

"That would be all right," Pete said from under the table, "maybe that way we'd win some of our money back."

"He was my one friend, my *only* friend," Frank reminded us, and went right on massaging. Yet more in sorrow than in hope of winning back his friend. He didn't give up till the pulmotor squad arrived. How they found out I still don't know. I think they just stopped in for a drink on the way home from some job and found another.

They tossed a coin, and the one who lost hauled the inhalator over to the shuffleboard.

"One side, buddy," he told Frank, but our Frank stood his ground. After all, he's from this neighborhood.

"Let him try, too, Frank," I told him. "We stand for fair play." Actually it wasn't fair play I wanted to see so much. It was just that it had been some time now since anyone raised anyone from the dead and I wanted to be on hand if it happened again.

But that Frank, he wouldn't give up. He went to the other side of the shuffleboard, yet he kept his hand on the old man's heart. I figured he figured that, if the

191

old man did come around, he'd get at least half the credit. If he had we would have given him all of it. After all, he's from this neighborhood.

"If you'd stop blowing cigar smoke in his face," the fireman told me, "he'd stand a better chance."

"Where does it say NO SMOKING?" I asked him to show me. Why should I take stuff off *him*?

After a time, the fireman took the head-piece off Joe's big blue nose and motioned to his friend at the bar. It was all over.

It took them a long time to get through the mob of kids in the door. It was a Spring night, and the kids wanted to see, but were afraid to come all the way in because it was a tavern.

But they made a path for some sort of serious little fellow with a black moustache. "I'm the doctor," he told us as if there were only one in the whole precinct.

Still, he must really have been a doctor at that, because he had a gold watch and didn't in the least mind showing it off. He listened to Joe's right wrist, gave it a bit of a shake, glanced at the watch, gave the left wrist a shake and looked at the watch again. He shook his head.

It isn't true what they say about pennies holding down a dead man's eyes, because they didn't hold down Joe's. Maybe he's got heavy eyes, I don't know, but the pennies kept rolling off. He tried half a dozen, but they'd slip and roll down the floor. Every time one passed the table I saw Pete's hand come out—there was one penny the doctor wouldn't see again.

"Try a dime," I told him to see if he would think that was heavier, and he did. When he lost that one I said, "Try a quarter."

"Give me two nickels," he told me, and two was just what I had. But I didn't get a dime for them. "The dime is under the table," he told me.

I wouldn't bend for it. I knew it was no use.

When he got the old man's lids closed under the nickels he wrote something in a little book, and left. "The boys will pick him up shortly," he told us.

What boys? The boys from the Royal Barons S.A.C.? They've buried a couple parties, but not officially.

"He meant the ambulance boys," Phil, the bartender, guessed. "You can't die in a public place unless you're a pauper. You got to go to a hospital to make it official."

"I think he meant the boys from Racine Street Station," Pete spoke up, and that sounded closest.

"Anyhow, say a prayer for the guy," Frank asked us, giving up his work at last. And began one himself—"Our Father who art in Heaven"—then the whiskey hit him and he couldn't remember the rest.

"Hollowed be Thy name," I remembered, and that was as far as I could go.

"Let's wait for the priest," I told Frank.

The kids in the doorway stood aside to let Father Francis through. He didn't look our way but we took off our caps all the same. He went right to the shuffleboard and did as fast and neat a job of extreme unction as if that old man were lying in bed. Someone brought an army blanket and covered the poor old stiff with that.

Father F. didn't look our way till he'd made the sign of the cross and pulled the blanket up. Then he came to where we waited.

"Oh, *Father*," Frank shouted like the priest had come just in time to save *him*. "I *forgot* the Lord's Prayer, Father."

"Remembering it isn't your trade," Father F. told Frank, "that's mine. Has the family been notified?"

Nobody had thought of that. But right away everyone wanted to be the first. John wanted to run straight to Joe's house, Sam said he'd phone. But Phil said, since it happened in his place, it was his job.

Then, it turned out, nobody knew where the old man lived or even what his full name was. Nobody had called him anything but Joe for years. Some said it was Wroblewski, some said it was Makisch, another said it was Orlov.

"Try looking in his wallet," somebody said from under the table.

Nobody had thought of that, either.

"Bring it to me, Frank," Father F. said.

"He was my one friend, let someone else," Frank declined.

Father F. went over and turned the blanket down and reached in and brought back Joe's wallet.

Joe's wallet, fat as leaves. But when he laid it on the bar it just lay there, so thin, so flat, so gone, it looked like it must have had some sort of little stroke of its own. When Father F. reached in, all there was was one thin single, nothing more.

Everybody pushed to see.

"What was he doing when he went?" Father wanted to know.

"Playing poker, Father," we told him.

"Penny ante?"

"Two-dollar limit."

"Put on Perry Como," I told one of the kids, because I didn't care how I spent just then.

Perry came on singing *Whither Thou Goest I Shall Go*. Oh, he sang it so easy, he sang it so free. And while he sang Phil poured a shot for John and a shot for me. He poured a shot for Father F. and a shot for Sam and a shot for Al and a shot for Frank. Then he poured a shot for himself and lifted his glass.

"To Joe, old Joe," he made a kind of toast.

"Oh, Frank," I heard a whisper from under the table. "How you massage! So *good*! How God is going to punish!"

The Pulpcon Kill

WILLIAM F. NOLAN

William F. Nolan is an authority on Black Mask magazine. His most recent book, The Black Mask Boys (1985), is what he calls a "historical anthology"—a collection of stories, each of which is preceded by an essay about the writer and his role in the development of what is now called the Black Mask tradition. "The Pulpcon Kill" evolved out of Nolan's research.

Like his Sam Space novels, about a tough, space-age private eye, "The Pulpcon Kill" pays humorous homage to the past masters of hard-boiled fiction. The story introduces a new private eye, Nick Challis, whose half-brother Bart was the detective in Nolan's first two mystery novels, Death Is for Losers (1968) and The White-Cad Cross-Up (1969).

William F. Nolan lives in California.

LATE. Beyond midnight. A twenty-four-hour Italian joint in the heart of New York. Big party. Mafia kingpin's birthday. Everybody laughing it up, drinking, singing off key, yelling at each other. The head honcho is Luigi somebody, and he's really zonked. Chug-a-lugging from a half-empty bottle of vino. Has a Sweet Young Thing on his lap. She's stroking his mustache and he's squeezing one of her boobs.

Outside, a misting rain makes the pavement shine. The street is quiet and dark. But you can see the party going on through the big plate glass window.

Three long, black limos, pebbled with rain, ease around the corner, rolling slow along the street. Their rear windows come whispering down as they near the twenty-four-hour joint and some shit-mean automatic weapons poke out.

The plate glass window explodes into jagged fragments as each limo glides past, cutting loose with enough firepower to win World War II. Total mayhem inside the Italian joint. Bullets cutting up chairs, walls and people. Luigi goes down in slow motion, gouting ketchup from a dozen wounds, the wine bottle splintering in his hand. . . .

I'd had enough. I got up and walked out. For one thing, I figured I'd seen the best part of the picture and, for another, the air conditioning unit was on the fritz and the theater was too damn hot.

It was a lot hotter outside on Ventura. The San Fernando Valley was having a real bitch of a September heat wave, with temperatures over 105, and some sticky humidity had been added to the package. Tropical storm off the Pacific was messing up the L.A. basin and the weather boys said it would last through the weekend.

I was in a bad mood. Muggy, excessive heat makes me tough to get along with. Result: a fight with the pneumatic red-haired flight attendant in Santa Monica. When she kicked me out of her condo I decided to take in the latest Bronson Mafia movie, just to cool off. Now I was hot and irritated. Figured I needed something cold inside me, so I drove down Ventura to Van Nuys, took a hard right up the alley behind the newsstand, and parked right under the "You Won't Believe It's Yogurt" sign.

Went inside. Ordered a two-scoop dish of coconut, with crushed chocolate-chip topping. The skinny college kid who worked there asked me how come I always ordered the same topping for my frozen yogurt when there were so many others to choose from. I thought that was a dumb question, so I didn't answer him.

I sat down at one of the little round butcher block tables and began spooning cold yogurt inside my hot stomach. Very soothing. My mood began to improve.

It was late afternoon and the place was nearly deserted. There was one other customer, a blue-eyed blond wearing shorts (with a particularly nice pair of legs inside them) and a splendidly packed T-shirt that said: WHAT YOU SEE IS WHAT YOU GET. She smiled across the room at me. "Are you Nicholas Challis?"

"Never call me Nicholas," I said. "Makes me sound like a Romanian prince—and that's not my image. How come you know who I am?"

"I know a lot more than that," she said, moving over to sit down at my table. Her no-bra act was terrific.

"What else do you know?"

"That you are thirty-two years of age, your father was Irish and your mother is a Mescalero Apache, and you have been a private detective for two years—since you moved here from San Diego after the death of your wife."

"Go on," I told her. "So far you're scoring 100 percent."

"You have a half-brother on your father's side who also works as a private investigator in the Los Angeles area. Your father is deceased, and your mother now lives in Albuquerque, New Mexico."

"Bet you don't know when I quit biting my nails," I said.

"Originally, you wanted to be a commercial artist, but you were not talented enough to make it work out financially. Your present office is located in Studio City here in the Valley and you don't smoke or have any children or pets. Shall I continue?"

"I don't see any reason to," I said. "You've obviously done a hell of a research job. The question is, why?"

"Let's go to my place and you'll find out. How does that sound?" And she gave me another flash of her perfect teeth.

"Sounds like I'm being seduced," I said. "And I'm always ripe for seduction." I stood up, leaving my yogurt. "I just hope your T-shirt is telling the truth."

It wasn't. What I saw I did *not* get, nor was I going to from what she told me once we were inside her

Malibu pad. All I got was her name: Charlene Vickers. The surf was doing its usual in-and-out number on the beach outside her picture window and Charlene was standing there looking at the afternoon ocean when she informed me that I had not been brought here for a romantic interlude.

"This is strictly business, Mr. Challis," she said. "I represent someone who urgently requires your services. He asked me to bring you here."

"I was hoping you were a P.I. groupie eager to partake of my sun-bronzed flesh," I said. "Instead, you want to put me to work. Doing what?"

"I'll let my employer tell you that."

"And who's your employer?"

"Frank Morrison. He's due here in exactly—" She checked a tiny gold pearl watch on her left wrist. "seven minutes."

"Great," I said. "I love split-second timing." I joined her at the window. The ocean was dead calm, with a few white sails edging the horizon. Clear day, no fog. "Just what is it that you *do* for Mr. Morrison? I mean, besides fetching lust-crazed private detectives to Malibu. Or shouldn't I ask?"

"I'm his live-in secretary," she said. "And you can make anything you want out of that." She said it coldly. In fact, she hadn't smiled since we'd arrived here. Once she'd dropped her yogurt act, she was just what she said, strictly business. Which depressed hell out of me. She looked like the Raintree Shampoo Girl and talked like Walter Mondale.

A car pulled into the gravel drive in front of the beach house. White 1955 T-Bird. In classic condition. Guy got out. Silver-gray crewcut. Not tall, but beefy. Wide chest and shoulders. Wearing a red-checked sport coat and matching slacks. Colorful.

He walked in and shook my hand, giving the bones a real workout. "I'm Frank Morrison," he said.

"No, you're not." I gave him a level stare. "You're Mickey Spillane."

He grinned at me. "Okay, so my full name is Frank Morrison Spillane—but I try to keep a low profile."

"Sure," I nodded. "By doing coast-to-coast beer commercials and playing your own character, Mike Hammer, in the movies."

"Guilty on the commercials, but I only played Hammer once, and that was back in the early sixties."

"I watch a lot of late night TV," I said.

Spillane walked over to Charlene, gave her a kiss on the cheek. Fatherly. Maybe she *was* his secretary.

"Get us a couple beers, doll."

She got two cans out of the fridge, gave me one. Spillane tabbed his open, took a long swig. Charlene poured herself some orange juice and we all sat down.

"I drink too much of this stuff," he said. "Gives you a big gut when you get older. And I'm no spring chicken." He belched. "But I work out, sweat it off."

"I'd like to get to the point," I said. "Why did you have me brought here?"

"Simple. To nail a creep who's been doing a number on me. He wants to shut off my juice."

"You talk like a comic strip," I told him.

"Hah!" Spillane chuckled. "That's where I got my start—with the comics. Used to write Captain America and Plastic Man. In the forties. Hammer came right out of that period. I wrote him as 'Mike Danger, Private Eye.' Planned to star him in his own comic book. But then I changed my mind and wrote him into *I, The Jury* as Mike Hammer. Did that first novel in just nine days. I write fast. And I'm not out to win the Pulitzer, I'm in it for the bucks." He scowled at me. "Anything wrong with that?"

I put up a hand. "Hey, I'm on *your* side."

He grinned. "I didn't mean to sound off—but I've taken a lot of hard raps for my stuff. From the critics. I don't know what the hell they expect! I write books and people buy 'em. It's just that simple."

"You say somebody's been after you? Threatening you?"

"More than just threats," Spillane said. He got up with his beer, began pacing the room. His heels rang on the polished hardwood floor. "About a month ago I came down here to film a commercial. From Big Sur, where I have a cabin. When I got here *this* was waiting for me."

The handwritten letter he handed over was addressed: *To a Thief.*

You have stolen from me. Through Kathleen, I know that all sins are punished. If not in this lifetime, then in the next. You will suffer bad karma for what you have done. I am here to serve cosmic justice. It is time for you to leave your present body, and I shall hasten your departure. Sum up your affairs. You have little time remaining.

And it was signed: *John D. Carroll.*

"You know the guy?" I asked Spillane, handing the letter back to him.

"Only John Carroll I ever knew was a film actor," he told me. "Used to work for the old Republic Studios in those sword-and-tit flicks. Haven't seen him for years. John's probably dead by now. But I know one thing. That's not his handwriting."

"A good chance the name's a phony," I said.

"In my game you get a lot of crazy mail," declared Spillane. "I ignored the letter, forgot about it. Two days later the phone rings and this wacko is on the line. 'I'm the man you robbed,' he says. 'Retribution is at hand.' And he hangs up."

"Is that all he said?"

"Yeah. Didn't bother to tell me what I'd robbed him of."

"You have any idea what he could be talking about?"

"Not a clue. But wackos don't need to make sense."

"What did you do?"

"Nothin' is what I did. But then, two days later, he calls again. And this time he says just one word: 'Tomorrow.' And hangs up."

"So?"

"So I didn't go out the next day. Stayed at my hotel. I own a .45 and I kept it out and ready. But nothing happened all day and I figured it was an empty threat." He took a final swig from the can, squeezed it double with one hand, tossed it into a wastebasket.

"Want another?" asked Charlene.

"Yeah," said Spillane. "How about you, Nick?"

"I'm fine. Got half the can left."

"Okay, so around eleven o'clock I drive down to an all-night market for a six-pack and just as I'm about to park on the lot somebody lets go with a pumpgun. Blamo! Took out the left side window. But I'd seen a flash of metal from the dark side of the building just before he'd fired. I ducked and floored the pedal. Really hot-assed it outa there!"

"Did you report it to the cops?"

"No, I just got the hell back to Big Sur. Then, this month, with more commercials pegged, I had Charlie here rent me this Malibu joint. So now I'm worried that this wacko will make another try for me."

"Have you heard from him this trip?"

"Not yet. But I expect to."

"I still don't see why you haven't called in some law."

"If I went to the cops on this they'd just tell me to wait till he takes another crack at me, then give 'em a ring. I could be stiffed by then! Also, I don't need any publicity right now. Like I said, outside of the commercials, I keep a low profile."

"You just might get your low profile blown away by Johnny-boy's popgun," I told him.

He squinted at me, gripping my left shoulder. "Look, I want *you* to find this psycho sonofabitch. I'll pay whatever it costs."

"Why me? There's a pisspot full of private investigators in L.A. with reps better than mine."

"Your brother recommended you," said Spillane. "Hell, Bart and I go way back. I wanted him to handle it, but he says he's leaving the detective game. Gettin' too old for blonds and bullets."

"Well, I can believe it about the bullets," I said.

"Speaking of bullets. . . ." Spillane gave me a hard look. "Do you pack heat?"

"When I have to," I said. "But I don't play it the way Bart does. He's the family gunslinger. Enjoys shooting people. I try to avoid doing that."

"Then you don't carry a piece?"

"Not on me, no."

"I make it you'll need one when you find this guy."

"Maybe," I said.

Spillane leaned forward to give me a flash of the .45 holstered under his left armpit.

I whistled. "Impressive."

"And I know how to use it."

"Obviously you're a lot tougher than I am," I said. "How come you don't go after this wacko yourself, with your big .45? Play Mike Hammer for real?"

"Hey, listen Buster, don't kid yourself—when I was younger I did my share of mixing it up with the bad guys." He was well into his second beer and pacing again, talking as he paced. "Even worked with the FBI to break a narco ring. That was a mean job, and I got the scars to prove it."

"So why hire me?"

"I'm like your brother. Gettin' too old for the rough stuff. Hell, I'll be sixty-seven next year. I need younger muscle."

He walked over to a desk, did some quick scribbling, and handed me a check. I looked at the sum, whistled again. It was a *fat* check.

"This should cover you for awhile. When you want more, give a yell. Money's no problem."

"I'll need that letter," I said. "It's the only thing I've got to work with."

He handed it over and we said our good-byes.

Charlene even smiled at me as I walked out the door.

First thing I did was run a computer trace on all of the John Carrolls in the L.A. area. Just in case the name might be legit. I found six John D. Carrolls, but there wasn't a psycho in the lot. Which proved that the would-be killer was using a phony name.

But sometimes you get lucky.

The creep's letter talked a lot about past lives—and it mentioned a "Kathleen." She could possibly be somebody who did regressions . . . guided people back into past lives.

It was a long shot, because Kathleen might have turned out to be the guy's wife or mother or girlfriend,

even his sister. But my gut said no, that she was someone who did this kind of thing for a living. A long shot,
like I said, but I played it out.

And got lucky.

I contacted a professor I knew at UCLA who was
into paranormal research and right away he brightened
when I asked him if he'd ever heard of anybody named
Kathleen who was into the past-life bag.

"Kathleen Jenks," he said. "She's done several hundred regressions. A very dedicated woman. And quite
friendly. You'll like Kathleen."

I nodded. "Where can I find her?"

"She works out of her apartment," he told me, looking up the address. It was on Harbor Boulevard in
Oxnard Shores, which is up the Ventura Freeway a
few miles beyond L.A. County.

I drove there after phoning for an appointment.
Told her I wanted to find out who I'd been in my last
life.

It was dark by the time I arrived.

A tall, rail-thin character was just leaving her place.
He gave me a long stare as we passed. Something
about the way his eyes looked told me I'd be seeing
him again.

I thumbed the buzzer and Kathleen Jenks opened
the door of her townhouse unit. One of four apartments in the building. She shook my hand, smiled, and
asked me to take off my shoes. "It's a house rule."

I followed her inside, carrying my shoes. My bright
Irish-green socks made me feel a little silly.

Kathleen was slim and small-boned, with hazel eyes

and dark waist-length hair that streamed thickly down her back. In her thirties, I guessed. Wore a long burgundy gown and had a kind of melodic voice, low-pitched and compelling.

She told me she'd been regressing people since 1974, and that she tape-recorded every regression. That interested me a lot.

"Was the guy I passed coming in here one of your clients?"

"That was Sam," she said. "I've regressed him several times. Quiet sort of fellow. But with a fascinating background. He was one of Napoleon's generals, you know. Died at Waterloo."

"Sorry to hear that," I said.

She smiled indulgently. "Death is never a thing to be sorry about; it's something to look forward to. It allows us to enter the next house in our universal cosmic journey."

"I never thought of it that way," I admitted.

Her apartment was jammed with books and seashells and mirrors and colored rocks and oil paintings and stained-glass globes. In the middle of it all was a huddled puffball of white fur with slitted black eyes.

"Her name is Shanti," said Kathleen, scooping up the cat. "It means 'peace' in Sanskrit. Say hello to the gentleman, Shanti."

The cat hissed at me.

"She's very tense around males. I'll put her in the kitchen. She won't bother us there." Kathleen moved toward the kitchen. "Why don't you go upstairs and lie down?"

"Huh?"

"That's how I conduct my regressions," she said. "With the subject lying down. There's a couch up there in the loft. Use that. I'll join you in a moment."

I climbed up to the loft, found the couch, and eased onto my back. She turned the lights off downstairs and came up carrying a hooded kerosene lamp and a notebook. "I use this to provide enough light for my notes," she told me.

She sat down cross-legged on a velvet pillow next to the couch, placing the lamp on the floor. I could smell the faint odor of kerosene. Then she switched on a tape recorder and arranged the open notebook in her lap.

"Would you prefer some white noise?" she asked.

I said "Huh?" again.

"A machine I can turn on. It blocks out the street noises. Some people are bothered by street noises."

"No, you can skip that. I'm fine."

"Well, then, are you ready?" she asked.

"I gotta warn you," I said. "I'm a tough subject to hypnotize."

"I don't hypnotize people. I try to induce an aura of inner peace, a kind of light trance state. Just close your eyes and allow my voice to guide you."

And she began to speak in a lilting flow, telling me how to relax the muscles in each section of my body. Then: "Imagine that you are in a small boat, on your back, under a serene blue sky, drifting endlessly down a wide stream. The sun is on the water, and the day is very peaceful. Your muscles are totally relaxed and your mind is open to the cosmic power of the water, carrying you back . . . back . . . back . . . through time itself, into another state of life, into. . . ."

"It's no good," I said, sitting up abruptly. "I have to be straight with you. I'm not here to take a boat trip into yesterday. I came here to get some info. In order to prevent a murder."

She gave me a penetrating look: "Are you with the police?"

"No, I'm a private investigator. I think you have vital information I need. On one of your subjects."

She switched off the recorder, stood up calmly. "Maybe we'd better go back downstairs."

"Yeah, maybe we'd better."

Like I said, sometimes you get lucky and this turned out to be one of my lucky nights. Yes, she *did* know a John D. Carroll. He'd told her he worked in a specialty shop, some kind of nostalgia place where they sell old pulp magazines and movie posters. She didn't know where the shop was located or where Carroll lived. He'd never given her an address or a phone number; he always called her for appointments. He'd come in several months ago for a past-life regression and they'd had maybe half a dozen sessions since then.

"But in all of them, he refused to be regressed beyond his last lifetime," she told me. "Most people who come to me want to reach back into as many of their past lives as possible. But John was fixated on this *one* prior life. He kept wanting me to explore more aspects of it. So I did."

"And what *was* he?" I asked. "In this other life."

"An author," she said. "He wrote thriller stories for the popular magazines of the period. Apparently he was quite successful at it, at least in the early years of his career into the 1940s."

"Did he write under another name—or did he use John D. Carroll?"

"That's all on the tapes. I don't recall the name he wrote under."

"I'd like to borrow those tapes. They could provide the information I need to run him down."

She stared at me; her eyes were cool. "I'm sorry, Mr. Challis, but these sessions are confidential. I never allow subject tapes to leave my possession."

"I can make it worthwhile," I said. "My client will pay whatever you ask."

"It's not a question of money, it's the principle. In a way, I am in the position of a priest in the confessional. I do not violate a subject's confidence."

"Look," I said firmly. "This guy is obviously insane. He's already made one attempt on the life of my client and he's sure to make another. You let me have those tapes and you'll be saving a man's life."

She thought about that for a long silent moment. Then she walked over to a tall bookcase on the back wall and ran her finger along a line of boxed tapes. Took out three, handed them to me.

"These are reel-to-reel," she said. "My player is broken at the moment or you could listen to them here. Have you a reel-to-reel machine?"

I nodded. "Got one in my office."

"Normally, I'd *never* do this," she said. "But in a case of potential homicide. . . ." Her voice trailed off.

"Believe me, you're doing the right thing," I assured her. "Can you tell me what Carroll looks like? You never said."

"Medium height and build. Thinning brown hair. Has a scar on his left cheek from a childhood accident."

"Age?"

"Well, he was born into his present body in 1959—which puts him in his mid-twenties."

"Does he have another appointment set with you?"

"No. I haven't heard from him for quite some time now."

I stepped to the door, opened it. A drift of cold night air reminded me we were near the ocean. "You may have saved a man's life. I thank you for all your help."

"You're quite welcome, Mr. Challis." There was a twinkle in her eyes. "But there are two important things you seem to have forgotten."

"Name them."

"Your shoes," she said.

I got back in my Honda and headed along Harbor toward the freeway. It was quiet, with no other cars on this section of the boulevard. A light rain began to patter against the window. I flipped on the wipers and reduced speed. No use taking chances. A thin drizzle like this can make the road damned slick.

Then I saw headlights coming up fast behind me.

Really fast. Had to be a road nut, driving at this rate in the rain. But my gut told me who it was.

John D. Carroll.

Maybe he'd spotted me coming out of Spillane's place in Malibu. At any rate, he'd followed me to Kathleen's and was closing in fast. To kill me.

Or was I getting paranoid? Could just be a coked-up high school kid out to impress his date with some hotshot driving. But the blast that took out the Honda's rear window told me it was Carroll.

Damn! My gun was in the office in Studio City. A million miles away.

Whatever he was driving, I figured I sure couldn't outrun him in a three-year-old Honda Civic with lousy rear shocks.

So what could I do? It would have to be something he wouldn't expect. I braked hard, sliding the Honda around into a full U-turn on the slick pavement, and headed right for him.

His lights filled my vision, two flaring circles of white fire, blinding me. I shaded my eyes from the glare with one hand, thinking, boyo, this is one hell of a gamble. I was counting on him to chicken out and swerve, maybe turn over in the wet, giving me the advantage.

But he didn't chicken out.

I was right on top of him.

We hit.

Not head-on. I wouldn't be telling about it if we'd hit head-on. We sideswiped each other in a grinding crush of metal, each of us caroming off to opposite sides of the boulevard.

I was okay. Not hurt, just shaken a little. I got the door open, climbed out fast, keeping low. My goal was the dark area between two apartment buildings fronting the boulevard. I had to get some cover and I had to get it quick.

As I ran, in a kind of half-crouch, I felt moisture on my forehead and upper lip. Not rain . . . sweat. My muscles twitched, anticipating a pumpgun charge between the shoulder blades, blowing my flesh apart. But that was in my mind. The guy didn't fire at me.

He had more important things to do.

From the darkness between buildings, I turned to see him getting the three tapes from the seat of my Honda . . . a medium-built guy in a long coat with what looked like a Winchester pump cradled under his left arm. I eased back into the shadows as he looked toward me. I could feel his eyes burning at me.

Then he got back in his car, a light tan Chevy, and motored away into the night.

But not before I was able to read his license number.

An hour later I was unlocking my office door in Studio City. I moved to the empty water cooler next to my desk and lifted the dusty belltop. Reached inside. Took out my Browning .380, checked the clip, then stuffed the automatic into my belt. One of these days I'd buy a holster. Or borrow one from Bart. Maybe he'd leave me his when he retired.

Then I walked back to the Honda, which was like me—battered but still operational—and drove out to the psycho's pad.

I'd gotten Dear John's address from a cop I knew. He ran the plate number for me. The Chevy was registered to one Franklin Elster Edwards. And he was clean. No wants, no warrants. Lived on Sunset Crest, up in the twisty hills above Mulholland Drive.

Edwards was obviously John D. Carroll's real name. Or else he'd stolen the car, which was unlikely since it wasn't listed on the hot sheet.

Mr. Edwards was not home when I got there. Driveway empty. No lights on inside. Everything churchyard quiet. I popped a rear lock and walked in, the .380 ready in my hand. Just in case.

The house was deserted. Nice little one-story joint, with dark Spanish furniture and lots of rugs. I poked around, opening drawers, checking things out. Didn't know what I was looking for, exactly. Until I found it.

A poem. On top of his desk in the den. And in the same handwriting as the letter he'd sent Spillane.

The thief will die
near the woods
While the Eye
is watching.

I phoned Spillane at the number he'd given me. Wasn't his Malibu place; it was the Marmont Hotel near the airport.

He answered on the first ring: "Yeah?"

"It's me. Challis. I've got a poem I want you to hear."

"*Poem?* You gone nuts?"

"This one is special. The wacko wrote it."

"Where the hell are you?"

"In a phone booth at a drugstore below Mulholland. I just left the guy's house. Wasn't home, so I had some time to look around."

"You got a name to give me?"

"Franklin Elster Edwards. Ring any bells?"

"Nope. What's been happening? How did you manage to find—"

I cut in. "Look, Mickey, I'll fill in all the details when I see you. But right now I think you'd better hear what this poem has to say."

"Okay, okay, so read the damn thing to me."

I did that. "What do you make of it?"

"Jeez." There was relief in his voice. "Takes a helluva load off my mind."

"How so?"

"Well, the 'thief' is me, natch. When he says I'll die 'near the woods' he means at my cabin in Big Sur. I live close to a wooded area. And the part about the 'Eye is watching' means you."

"Why me?"

"He figures I'll be taking you with me as my bodyguard when I leave L.A. He plans to snuff me at the cabin, with you, the private eye, 'watching.' Simple."

"Meaning he won't try to make another hit in this area."

"That's it. He's gonna wait until I go back to Big Sur."

"Which you *won't* do."

"Damn right, I won't. Not till we drop a net over this guy. But I'm telling you, Nick, it's a load off my mind. I've been sleeping with a gun under my pillow."

"Our friend has no way of knowing we've scanned his little poem," I said. "Probably wrote it to amuse himself. I left it right where I found it, on his desk. So now it's just a matter of rounding him up."

"Can you do that, or do you want the cops in on it?"

"At this point, I think we need some law. I hope to keep you out of it. At least for now. I can charge him with attempted murder. He tried to gun me tonight."

"I thought you said he wasn't home?"

"It was earlier. You'll hear the whole scam when we get together. Right now, I'd better get the cops onto this guy."

"Will you do one more thing for me first?" asked Spillane. "I'm a little worried about Charlie."

"What's wrong with her?"

"Maybe nothing. But I've been phoning her out at Malibu. No answer. I figure that maybe she—"

"Christ!" I yelled. *"That's* where he went after our little road encounter!"

And before Mickey could say anything more I slammed down the phone, jumped into the Honda and headed hell-bent for Malibu.

When I drove slowly past the house along Pacific Coast Highway I couldn't see any lights inside. But I was getting only a partial view from the road. Still it was enough to concern me.

I parked on the dirt shoulder, avoiding the half-circle of crushed gravel that angled from the highway down to the front of the house. If the creep was there I didn't want to announce my arrival.

The tan Chevy wasn't anywhere in sight, but that could mean he was playing it as cautiously as I was. I came in from the patio, gripping the .380 so tightly my fingers were cramping. Nerves. You never get used to being shot at, and it had already happened to me once that night. A Winchester pump is a mean piece of iron; blows a hole in you wide enough to see the stars through.

I could smell the ocean, like a big wet animal nuzzling the beach. The night breeze off the water had a sharp edge to it.

There was no light or movement downstairs. The pull drapes were open and I had a clear view of the rooms. No sign of any kind of struggle. And as quiet as the dark side of the moon. Maybe Charlene was asleep upstairs. Maybe I was wrong to be worried. My nerves eased down.

I came in from the porch through the sliding glass door, which was unlatched. The first bad sign. It *should* have been latched.

I got nervous again.

The stairs were next on the agenda, and I sweated a

lot going up. Topside, I heard a muffled whimpering. Like a child having a nightmare.

The door to the main bedroom was ajar when I eased in, crouching, the automatic poised in my hand. I hoped to God I wouldn't find the psycho waiting for me in the dark.

I didn't.

Charlene was inside, alone. Tied and gagged on the bed. Wearing a torn pink nightrobe. Behind the gag, she whimpered, her eyes wide and desperate.

I put away my .380 and switched on a bed lamp. Then I moved to free her. "Take it easy, you're okay now," I said. Poor kid. I could see she had the shakes.

I stripped the gag from her mouth, cut loose her wrists and ankles. She fell forward across the bed into my arms, sobbing deeply, her whole body shaking.

"He . . . he was here!" She gasped out the words. "For almost an hour. It was horrible!"

"Did he hurt you?"

"No, but he forced me to . . . to . . ."

"Have sex with him? Did the bastard *rape* you?"

"Not that. He forced me to listen—while he read to me."

"He *what?*"

"Read to me." She was chafing her wrists to restore circulation. "He told me he needed a witness, someone who would testify that his claim was legitimate. About being stolen from." She drew in a long shuddering breath. "So he read to me, from his stories, to prove his claim."

"What kind of stories?"

"They were all private eye things. From old pulp magazines. About a crude detective named Race Williams who carried two big .45s and was always shooting someone in the head with them. And beating up people. The guy showed me his byline on each one. He was very proud of his byline being on them."

"John D. Carroll?"

The lamplight haloed her blond hair as she shook her head. "No, they were all by Carroll John Daly. He said he used John D. Carroll only once—for one story —but that it was a good name to hide behind. He didn't want the public to know who he was until after Mickey was dead."

"What, exactly, did he say Mickey had stolen from him?"

She looked at me, eyes intense. "His style . . . all the violence and the beatings . . . he swore that Mike Hammer was really Race Williams and that Mickey had made millions by using *his* detective, and that *he* had died broke."

"*Died?*"

"You know, in his life before this one."

"Wow," I said softly.

"He's convinced that in his new body he has this cosmic duty to avenge his other self—the one who died back in 1958."

"The guy obviously has a lot of rungs missing in his ladder," I said. "Every writer starts with a role model, another writer he likes to read. And Mickey was probably influenced by Daly's work. But that's a long way from outright theft."

"Not to this guy, it isn't," she said.

"How *was* his stuff—the stories he read from?"

A smile bloomed on her face. That special smile. "It was all terrible crap," she said.

I phoned my cop friend and had him put out an A.P.B. for the wacko. Then I poured Charlene a Scotch rocks, another for me. We were feeling warm and relaxed, knowing it was over, that they'd pick up the guy soon, probably back at his place on Sunset Crest.

"You did a brave thing tonight, Nick," she told me. "Coming through that bedroom door to help me, not knowing if the creep was still in here with his gun aimed at you. He could have blown you in half."

"Stupid is what it was, not brave. But when I heard you whimpering I just *had* to find out if you were okay. I'm just glad he wasn't still around."

"That makes two of us," she said softly, leaning toward me and kissing me on the chin, cheeks, forehead. Little sex kisses. Meant to arouse me.

I was aroused.

We were downstairs, on one of the thick rugs, with a fire going. She looked great in her pink robe by firelight.

I put down my Scotch, reached for her, folding her tightly into my arms. She felt even better than she looked.

"Remember my T-shirt?" she said with a cat's smile.

"Who could forget it?"

"Well . . . what you see is what you get."

And she slipped out of the robe.

Sometimes, being a lust-crazed private detective has its advantages.

We phoned Mickey at the hotel to let him know Charlene was okay, and he said for us to come on over. He was shooting a commercial at the Marmont, and we could all have a long talk after he finished.

"I thought they shot commercials in the daytime," I said.

"They do, but this one is special. We gotta do it tonight because of the background."

"Costs more, doesn't it?"

"A bundle. The crew's on golden time. But I let my producer worry about cost. I'm just a hired hand. You coming on over?"

"Sure," I said. "Wouldn't miss it."

At the Marmont, the desk clerk told us that Mr. Spillane was in the Red Room, "with all those pulpcon freaks."

I arched an eyebrow. "Pulpcon? What's that?"

"Pulp magazine convention—where all these freak-type collectors meet to swap issues and gas it up about the grand old pulp days. They have a big get-together each fall and this year they picked *this* hotel for their weirdo shindig."

Suddenly I turned as green as my socks and pulled

the .380 Browning from my belt. "The poem! Mickey was all *wrong* about the poem!"

"Nick! What's happened?" Charlene was staring at me, wide-eyed, like the desk clerk.

"You know the poem I quoted to Mickey. I told you about it. . . ."

"Yes, but—"

"Those old magazines were made from *wood*pulp— and *that* was what he meant when he said 'the thief will die near the woods.' He didn't mean Big Sur. And when he said 'while the Eye is watching,' he meant the *camera* eye! That psycho's going to blow Mickey away during the beer commercial!"

And I took off for the Red Room at full gallop.

Franklin E. Edwards, alias John D. Carroll, alias Carroll John Daly, was off to one side of the big convention room, standing behind a red velvet-covered pillar, his Winchester aimed at Mickey, who was holding up a beer can and grinning for the camera when I came through the wide oak-and-brass swing door like a bull into a china shop, knocking six startled pulp collectors flat on their asses.

The place was jammed with addicts poring over piles of flaking yellowed magazines stacked on some two dozen large display tables across the room—but I spotted our boy instantly, dropped to one knee, and squeezed off a round. And another. And another. Missing him with all three shots.

I was nervous.

Edwards swung the pumper in my direction and blew two crystal lamps that were set into the flocked-velvet wall above my head into tiny glittering pieces. Guess he was a little nervous himself.

Then with everybody yelling and stampeding, with tables falling and magazines fluttering, Edwards darted through a side door, me right after him, and sprinted up a short flight of stairs to a freight elevator. I got there just as the sliding door shut, but I could guess where he was headed.

Straight for the hotel roof.

I caught the next elevator and followed him up there, snapping a fresh clip into the Browning.

After I'd ducked out of the elevator and taken a dive behind a large standing air vent, the roof got very, very quiet. In all the Red Room confusion my gun-happy friend had made a clean getaway. Apparently I was the only one to follow him up here.

Which was an unsettling thought.

Here we were, me with my .380 pea-shooter, which suddenly felt very small in my fist, against a killer with a cannon powerful enough to blow away half the building. I'd robbed him of his cosmic destiny, and I knew he was plenty pissed.

Nicky boy, I said to myself, you have royally screwed up. There's a good chance you are going to leave this hotel with no head.

A mothering big 747 made a lot of noise then, coming in low for its landing approach at LAX, going over us like the wrath of God. The whole roof vibrated.

When things had quieted down again I tried a yell: "Give it up, Edwards! The cops are on the way. Put down that Winchester and come out with your hands in the air where I can see 'em and you won't get hurt."

This was prime bull and we both knew it. I wasn't going to hurt him; he was going to hurt *me*.

And when the air vent blossomed into sudden shell-burst fragments in front of me I knew I was right. The concussion knocked the .380 out of my hand. It ricocheted across the roof, hitting the psycho's shoe.

He stood up, into the light, maybe ten feet in front of me, with the round black mouth of that Winchester aimed at my belly. He pumped the weapon, setting it up for the shot.

"Oh, shit," I said.

There was no place to hide. It was time for me to enter private eye heaven.

Which was when Sam showed. I saw him crawl out of an open glass skylight directly behind the psycho, saw him raise the short-barrel Colt .45 he was packing and cock it.

The psycho spun at the sound. Brought up his gun. But not fast enough.

A round from the Colt took his head apart.

Sam walked over to me.

"I've seen you before," I said. "Earlier tonight. Leaving Kathleen's apartment."

"Right," he said. "I was tailing our friend here. But I lost him out on Harbor Boulevard. That was embarrassing because I'm a pretty fair shadow man. Usually I don't lose people."

"How long have you been following him?"

"Ever since the day I spotted that Winchester pump in the back seat of his car. Then there was something about his eyes. Aroused my suspicious nature."

"You a cop?"

"Nope. I'm an insurance salesman. But I used to be a Pink."

"A Communist?"

He chuckled. "A Pinkerton detective. Last time I worked that game was in the early twenties back in Frisco. Long time ago."

"You don't look that old."

"I'm not. Not in this life. Ask Kathleen about me sometime. She'll tell you my story."

"Who are you?"

"You mean, who *was* I. That's more important."

"Who then?"

"When I was a Pink they called me Sam. I never used my middle name till I became a writer. I mean, who the hell ever heard of a Pink named Dashiell?"